Young Man
with a Horn

A Houghton Mifflin
Literary Fellowship Book

Young Man
with a Horn

by Dorothy Baker

SENTRY EDITION

Houghton Mifflin Company
The Riverside Press Cambridge
1961

TO
RAYMOND BRANSON DODDS
AND
ALICE GRADY DODDS

THE inspiration for the writing of this book has been the music, but not the life, of a great musician, Leon (Bix) Beiderbecke, who died in the year 1931. The characters and events of the story are entirely fictitious and do not refer to real musicians, living or dead, or to actual happenings.

"Prologue"

~~~~~~~~~~~~~~~~~~~~~~~~~~~~~~~~~~~~

WHAT I'm going to do is to write off the story of Rick
Martin's life, now that it's all over, now that Rick is
washed up and gone, as they say, to his rest.

There isn't much to it, in its bare outline. Rick was
born in Georgia five or ten minutes before his mother
died and some ten days before his father checked out
and left him with his seventeen-year-old aunt and her
brother. These two worked their way to Los Angeles
eight years later and brought him with them; and there
he grew up in the way he apparently had to go. He
learned to play the piano by fooling around with pianos
in churches and roadhouses — any place, in fact, where
there was a piano that could be got at and fooled around
with. And because he had right in his bones whatever
it takes to make music, he became while he was still a
kid a very good pianist. But a piano wasn't exactly
right for him, and he turned to brass finally; he earned
enough money to buy himself a horn. And then he

learned to play a horn — a trumpet, if there's anybody here who doesn't know what kind of a horn a horn is — and that was his proper medium. He learned a lot from Art Hazard, the great negro trumpeter, but that doesn't explain what made him so good.

He played in five- and six-piece bands around Los Angeles, and one day he was discovered for what he was worth by Lee Valentine, who could scarcely believe his ears. Valentine, playing a cross-country tour of moving-picture houses, had been put on Rick's trail by Jeff Williams, the negro band leader, who had known Rick as a boy in Los Angeles and had kept him in mind as a future bright light for a good white band. Lee Valentine didn't need to be told twice; he signed Rick and took him back to New York with the band.

He was a sensation, particularly among musicians. He was such a sensation that it wasn't long until Phil Morrison, who ran the best big orchestra of the day, bought him, and then he continued to be a sensation for Mr. Morrison. He loved his work. He had something and he knew it. He never got tired, kept it up night after night, and after he got through with the night's dance he'd get together with other men from other bands who were interested in seeing how far they could go, and then he'd really play the rest of the night.

He pushed it too far. He didn't sleep and he didn't eat, because he could do so many other things. He could drink, for instance, and before he knew it he was drinking almost constantly in order to keep everything else going. It didn't work out that way, however, and he finished up his time in this life before he was thirty. He was mourned, I might add, by almost nobody except me and two negroes, Jeff Williams and Smoke Jordan. There was a woman, named Amy North, but there's no telling how she felt about it. I dare say Rick's death was regretted by musicians here and there, but it will only be a question of time until he's forgotten completely. One of these days even his records will be played out and give forth nothing but scratching under a steel needle. When that time comes Rick Martin will really be dead, dead as a door-nail, and I hate to see it happen.

That's the story, and it could never be called a grand tragic theme; it does not depict the fall of a noble person from high to low estate — Rick Martin never got anywhere near high estate, though he did make a lot of money for a while. But it is a story that has the ring of truth and an overtone or two. It is the story of a number of things — of the gap between the man's musical ability and his ability to fit it to his own life; of the difference between the demands of expression and the demands of life here below; and finally of the difference between good and bad in a native American art form — jazz music. Because there's good in this music and there's bad. There is music that is turned out sweet in hotel ballrooms and there is music that comes right out of the genuine urge and doesn't come for money.

The story ends with death. Our Mr. Martin, from the moment he began fooling around with pianos, was riding for a fall. I shouldn't have said fooling, because he wasn't fooling; he meant it. In Rick Martin's music there was, from the first, an element of self-destruction. He expected too much from it and he came to it with too great a need. And what he expected he never quite found. He might have found it in another kind of music, but he had no training or any way of coming to know another kind of music. So he stuck to jazz and to the nervous, crazy life that goes with it. And he made a good thing of it; he made an amazing thing of his own playing; he couldn't even keep pace with it himself. He was, in his way, like Tonio Kröger, Mann's inspired and bewildered poet, who 'worked not like a man who works that he may live; but as one who is bent on doing nothing but work; having no regard for himself as a human being but only as a creator.'

Now these are strong words and should surely apply much more truly to a poet like Tonio Kröger than to the man who played hot trumpet in Phil Morrison's band. But I don't think they do, and that's the thing about Rick's story that moves me. The creative urge is the creative urge, no matter where you find it. Rick did what he could do so well that I, for one, won't be likely ever to hear his name without feeling my hair rise.

But if you choose to look at it this way, you have to go easy or somebody will say you're arty. Dance music should be criticized in its own terms, and its own terms are such inbred shop-talk that no one outside the trade could understand them. How could you say what it was that Rick had and what he stood for without getting out of bounds in one way or another?

You could, of course, twist Rick's life into a fiction and write off a clear-cut commercial story about a good-looking young man who went to a good school and then, being musically inclined, went to New York and joined a big-time dance band. You could have him smoke Marihuana once or twice, just for the hell of it; and tell whom he loved and all the rest of it. He could be playing at one of the place-names of capitalism, say the Waldorf-Astoria, and between dance sets he could meet the daughter of some kind of magnate, and it would be love and our man would never have to play another night's dance music, but just lie happily married on the deck of his wife's yacht night after night for the rest of his life, which would be protected and long.

But this can't be that. This one has to be the story of a young man who, without even knowing what it was, had a talent for creating music as natural and as fluent as — oh, say Bach's. Rick Martin never would be put down to playing exactly what was written for him; he'd just sit there and fit himself into the heavy going, but when his own turn came, or whenever he saw his chance, he would take off and invent, extempore, some of the freshest, most imaginative music that ever occurred to anyone.

Our man is, I hate to say it, an artist, burdened with that difficult baggage, the soul of an artist. But he hasn't got the thing that should go with it — and which I suppose seldom does — the ability to keep the body in check while the spirit goes on being what it must be. And he goes to pieces, but not in any small way. He does it so thoroughly that he kills himself doing it.

Book One

Book One

IN THE first place maybe he shouldn't have got himself
mixed up with negroes. It gave him a funny slant on
things and he never got over it. It gave him a feeling
for undisciplined expression, a hot, direct approach, a
full-throated ease that never did him any final good in
his later dealings with those of his race, those whom
civilization has whipped into shape, those who can contain themselves and play what's written. But whether
he should have or shouldn't have doesn't matter much
now.

He lived in Los Angeles from the time he was eight
years old — in a part of Los Angeles that was not
notably class-conscious, or indeed conscious of anything.
He lived in an apartment with his aunt and uncle
(brother and sister, not husband and wife) and he had
a bed of his own in an empty storeroom down the hall.
He was alone a good share of the time. His uncle
worked in a meat-packing plant and his aunt worked

in a pants factory. He got, when the occasion demanded
and other things worked out right, some nice pants out
of his aunt's job, and his uncle paid the rent and bought
part of the food. Neither aunt nor uncle was home more
than a night or two a week. They led their own lives.

Rick, on the other hand, was almost always at home.
He read library books constantly and indiscriminately.
He read them fast, one after another, and subject-
matter was beside the point. It was as if he'd been told
that if he didn't read at least one book a day — any
book — something pretty bad would happen to him.
And it would have. If he hadn't kept himself busy
reading, he'd have worried himself sick about how he
hardly ever went to school and about what would
happen to him when he did show up again.

The truth is, anybody who knew him would tell you
the same thing, that he just wasn't very bright in school
— he never could remember, off-hand, what seven times
seven mounts up to. He wasn't especially good at putting his finger on the spot where the Nile rises, either,
or at saying with any conviction which way it flows
and which lands it drains; and he wouldn't even make
a guess at how many cubic feet of sediment it leaves
around on the delta in a year's time. He had the same
trouble with the Mississippi, what's more. He could
memorize like a flash, though. That is, he could memorize anything that had any swing to it, anything that
he could take hold of rhythmically. But it didn't help

him to get along any better. The time his teacher
assigned the first stanza of 'The Children's Hour' to be
memorized by the next day, he read through the whole
poem four or five times and there he had it. And the
next day everything went fine for a while; he stood up
in his turn and recited the first stanza faultlessly, only
he forgot to stop there; he went right through the
second stanza and was warming up to the third when
the teacher said, 'Sit down. You must have learned
it in some other school.'

That's how it went all through grammar school; he
couldn't seem to get off on the right foot. He wasn't
tough, he was well-mannered enough, but he just
couldn't seem to get going and it got harder and harder.
They graduated him in spite of it. They graduated
everybody in spite of things. It wasn't a strong school
scholastically; the Mexicans couldn't learn English,
and the niggers played around too much, and the
Americans didn't seem to have the right background.
The Japanese, though; the Japanese were smart as a
whip, bright as a dollar. They were, in a body, magna
cum laude at graduation. And Rick's aunt swiped him
a pair of white pants for it.

High School, which should have been better, was
worse. The first year of high school differed from the
last year of grammar school in one important respect:
Rick quit staying home to read library books and
began, instead, to hang around the All Souls' Mission,

on Washington just below Central Avenue, monkeying with the piano. It started on his first day in high school. He had a bad time getting registered. He stood almost all day in a hall in front of the principal's office, and when his turn came he became utterly confused. He listened to the jargon — major subjects, minor subjects, required subjects, physical education, manual training — with a polite ear but no understanding. And then, finally, the principal, or it may have been just the faculty adviser, came to the point. The point was that a student should decide right now the way he wanted his life to go. He could take, for example, a commercial course — typing, shorthand, bookkeeping, and the rest, and go into commerce; he could pick a vocation — automobile mechanics, radio, woodwork, what-not (they've got a course called Cosmetology at the same school now, but they didn't know about that then. Even marcelling hadn't gained any real ground). Or, if the student wanted to elect a profession — medicine, the law, the church, teaching, or whatever other professions there are, what he'd better do was take a general college preparatory course. And Rick, intent on making a good impression, said right out of a clear sky, 'I'll take that one.'

'Which?' asked the guide.

'The college general,' said Rick handsomely, and the adult wrote it off: Edward Richard Martin, general college preparatory.

'That's all, then, Edward; be in room 200 on the second floor tomorrow morning at half-past eight.'

Rick went away. He knew he'd made another false start and he loosely considered going back, admitting the fraud, and signing up for an honest trade like a man. He walked slower and slower, and when he got to walking so slowly that he was no longer moving, he looked up and saw: ALL SOULS' MISSION. ENTER. REST AND PRAY.

He entered. No one was there. It was just a big room with a lot of backless benches, a pulpit, and, over in one corner, an upright piano. Rick sank to a bench, grabbed up a hymnal, and began to read as fast as he could at the first place he opened, which happened to be the index. It didn't make good reading; it only quoted part of the title of the hymn and then gave the page:

Every Day I Need..... 7
In the Sweet.......... 43
Will There Be Any.....202.

There was nothing there to take his mind off his troubles, and so he turned to another part of the book and began to sing number 14 note by note. That was one thing he'd picked up in grammar school; he could read music like a flash, treble clef, bass clef, anything at all. When he'd found the tune, he stopped singing notes and sang words, but the words were so silly that even he couldn't stay with them, and then it occurred to him to see if it would work out on the piano.

It worked out, all right. It started to work itself out that very day. Rick stood there, head on one side, forehead in pleats, figuring it out. And after a while he dragged up one of the benches vertical to the piano, and sat on the end of it. He stayed there until dark, and I can scarcely believe it myself, but the story goes that he could play the piano by dark; he could play number 14 on the piano by dark. He couldn't find the light switch, then, and so he went home and went right to bed, so that he could think about just how it was that he had done it, and how maybe it might sound better if he made a change or two here and there.

And the next day he didn't show in room 200 on the second floor at half-past eight. He was in All Souls' at seven-thirty, and glad to be there.

2

It seems wrong that the thing worked out that way. You would think that Edward Richard Martin, just as a matter of course, just as a normal thing, would have turned up on time at Lowell High School nearly every morning, and being what he was, a decent, sensitive, and fairly thoughtful boy, he would have worked up an interest in *Ivanhoe* or the *Classic Myths*, or he might have got good at figuring out Latin constructions or chemical formulae — something or other would have smiled at him, and he'd have gone through high school and worked his way through college and come out to face the world with that special assurance that college graduates used to face the world with. He might even have gone into the brokerage business and cleaned up. Plenty of assured young men were cleaning up in the brokerage business at precisely the time Rick would have been right to go into it. You'd certainly think something would have happened, just simply as a matter of course, to have turned him toward a workaday way of life, the normal, childlike, innocent life that politicians, say, or say engineers, lead. At the very least, if he'd stuck to his guns and gone through school he could have got on in a Standard Oil station; he was good-looking enough.

But that's just one way, and a wrong one, of looking at it. He might have, if he'd stayed around schools and the right people had happened to get interested in him (a service that the teaching profession performs fairly regularly) — he might have become what he almost was, a man who had something important to say.

The fact that he didn't turn up at Lowell High School for almost a year, and then under a compulsion that made it impossible for him to do anything but cut loose again, makes speculation useless.

What he did do was fine, in itself; you can say that, at least. It's pretty sweet to think about a boy, just turned fourteen, being at All Souls' Mission every day, sometimes as early as six in the morning, working out on the upright in the corner and looking not unlike St.

Cecilia, only blond and smaller and thinner in the face. Looking not at all like St. Cecilia, in fact, but giving the same impression of being busy with music.

He was completely one-track. He sat there and took them one by one. When he had one down, he'd open the hymnal to another place, at random, and start another one. This random choosing was the only element of chance in his method. The rest of it was routine that he developed in the first three days and never swerved from thereafter. First he played through the hymn with his right hand — the vocal part — to fix the tune in his mind; then he'd take it measure by measure: right hand alone, left hand alone, then fit them together and keep it up, over and over, until it was perfectly all right to go on to the next measure. And when each single measure had been done that way, he'd go through the whole thing, over and over until it was right. At first it took him about two days to a hymn, and then when he began to spot frequent combinations it didn't take so long. In a month's time he had it down to about one an hour. And then he stopped the random opening and began to pick and choose; he had come to see that some of the hymns had a kind of style to them that others missed. He found one, for instance, that looked a lot simpler than it was. It was called 'Adeste Fideles,' and it took him the better part of two days to make it come out; but when he had it he liked it the best of the lot, notwithstanding the outlandish title.

It was only by the purest good fortune that he didn't happen to run into any of the All Souls' crowd any sooner than he did. He didn't even try to avoid them; it never occurred to him after he got interested in finding out how to play a piano that the mission was anything but a room with a piano in it. But it was. They had meetings there a couple of nights a week and all day and most of the night Sunday. Rick missed them Sundays because his aunt and his uncle were usually at home and he thought he ought to stay around. And he was never there at night because he had never found out how to turn the lights on.

But that kind of thing couldn't last forever, and it didn't. Late one afternoon five or six of them, early comers, came in on him and made quite a to-do about finding him there. Not that they were displeased about it; on the contrary, they were tickled to death. Rick was sitting at the piano, playing along very nicely, and he didn't even hear them come in. He had his head on one side and his mouth pursed, and his hair was bright from the last of the sun that came through the window in a single, concentrated beam. To one practiced in hallucination the beam might conceivably have looked like a halo. It was enough for this crowd, in any event. They got the idea, being hipped, as they were, on religion, that Rick was an angel, and not only that but that he'd been put down in All Souls' for a reason — very possibly to give them some advance information on the Second Coming. They proceeded, on that assumption, to try to get some kind of Message out of him. They were all pretty well lit with whatever it is that cults of that kind always seem to get hold of, and they got fairly rough with Rick, each one eager to get the story first. They made a tremendous noise, considering that there weren't very many of them, and for Rick it was like being awakened from a sweet sleep by marauders.

They were a notorious group, the All Souls, and their creed was a nice blend of spiritualism, holy-rolling, direct communion, and exorcism. In fact they had once been hauled up in a body for questioning after they had attempted to exorcise one of their number by flagellation. They literally beat the devil out of the fellow and he died. The case was dismissed, finally, for lack of evidence, the Souls being able, when the occasion demanded, to keep very quiet. It was nice for Rick that he didn't know this story; he was scared silly as it was. He couldn't say a word in the way of a message, and they, for their part, lost interest in him and began making up their own messages. Finally the whole thing broke up into aimless and unreasonable yelling around: 'Praise the Lord, I've led a wicked life.'

Rick got hold of himself after a long time of it. He tried the simplest of ruses and it worked. He went up to one of the women, the one who seemed to be the ringleader, and said politely and confidentially, 'Pardon me a minute; I'll be right back,' and got out. He ran all the way home and intended to sleep with his uncle. The only thing that kept him from it was that his uncle didn't come home.

3

AFTER that Rick had the fear of the Lord in him. He was lost and wandering with nothing now to do, now that the All Souls' upright was out. It was a question, for him, of going back to school and working his head off to catch up after he'd been told off for six weeks' delinquency, or of shutting himself up at home with library books, or of doing the impossible: going back to the mission, taking a chance on another run-in with the Souls and playing their piano in spite of them. There was no satisfactory choice to make here. Reading wouldn't hold him any more, and it was sort of late to go back to school — even the Mexicans can beat you out with a six weeks' handicap, and the Japanese were probably on the point of graduating again. And the All Souls' Mission was so much poison now. He couldn't get within a mile of it without having his liver go white as a sheet. Three choices, and not one he could choose.

So he followed the course that offered least resistance to his interest. He hung around pawnshops eyeing portable musical instruments and trying to figure out, through the window, just how you'd go about getting from one note to the next on a clarinet. And when he thought he understood it, he went on to the study of the trumpet (there were five in the window), but it was a much harder instrument to play by eye. There are eight tones in a scale and only three things to push on a trumpet. He gave it up, finally; at least he decided to wait until a time when he could get his hands on a trumpet and find out for himself. He thought of hocking something and getting himself one; in point of fact, that's all he did think of, but the only plan that looked good to him — that of hocking library books — he had to abandon as impracticable. He had, at that time, four pairs of pants, each one as good as the last, and three very tricky hangers for them, but he wouldn't allow himself to think of hocking his pants; his aunt had to put herself to so much trouble to get them for him. No more could he hang around the streets all the time with his nose against pawnshop windows. They throw you in for that kind of thing; that's vagrancy. Worse still in Rick's case, it was vagrancy and truancy, the kind of thing they haul you back to school for. He knew without being told.

And then, all at once, it occurred to him that the smart thing to do would be to get a job and earn enough money to retire to his uncle's apartment with a clarinet or a trumpet honestly paid for and take up his studies where he had left off. Easiest thing in the world to pick up a hymnal some place; All Souls' isn't the only church in Los Angeles. Easiest thing in the world to pick up some sheet music too, if you knew where some was.

He was little, though; at fourteen he looked ten, and not such a strong ten either. He might have got on in a boys' choir — that's about the only job he'd have been right for — but there weren't any boys' choirs. There was, on the other hand, a fight arena in that part of town, and he went there to ask about selling programs and near beer on fight nights. He didn't get the job. He knew it before he asked. He had been too much indoors and too little nourished and he bore precocious scars of contemplation; and with these items lined up against him it was impossible for anyone to expect him to develop the aggressiveness and low-down optimism so necessary to the salesman. Same thing next door at the gymnasium of Harry Beavers. Rick stood around, and after a while Beavers himself came up to him and said, 'What do you say, kid?' And when Rick had said it, Beavers gave him a friendly grin and said: 'Tell you what I'll do. If we ever need a man to throw in a sponge I'll phone you up.'

And then, when things were looking the very worst, a job fell bang in his lap. He went downstairs to Gandy's Pool Hall, Billiards, Snooker, and Bowling, one noon to get himself a chocolate bar, and even as he chose it he saw a sign inside the showcase: Boy Wanted. He bought his bar, put it in his pocket, and walked across the room to calm down. Then he went back and said to the man behind the counter (it was Gandy himself), 'Do you still want a boy?'

That was about all there was to it. He went right to work. All he had to do was set up tenpins in one alley while they were being knocked down in the other alley, and then set them up in the other alley while they were being knocked down in the one he'd just finished setting them up in, and repeat. The kid that had the job before Rick, Gandy told him, wasn't paying attention to his business one day and he sort of got his leg hurt, so watch them balls, see, we're not liable.

Nice work and two-fifty a week for it, twenty dollars for two months, forty for four, and taper off from there; quit and buy anything you like, just like finding it. Meanwhile, watch those balls.

4

EDWARD RICHARD MARTIN got along fine with his work. At least he kept his job. He set them up in the other alley very nimbly, he didn't let himself get bowled over, and he drew his pay every Saturday night, two-fifty right in his hand. And besides that, it was at Gandy's that he met his first friend, Smoke Jordan — his first, last, and always friend, Smoke.

Smoke Jordan worked at Gandy's off and on; he swept out and mopped up. He had had Rick's job, too, a long time before, but the bowling trade kept falling off and Gandy figured it out finally and ended by hiring

a shorter and less deliberate pin-setter. Smoke was
eighteen, easy six feet tall, and on the dark side between
oxblood and midnight blue, a good deep color with fine
high lights in it. He was a thoughtful boy, inclined to
philosophy, and his movements were precise and slow.
Gandy didn't give him credit for being all there, but he
was wrong. Smoke was slow, but he had a reason for it.
The way he walked, that slow drag, might have looked
offhand to be simply the gait of the shiftless, but if
you'd really watch him walk, judgment suspended,
you'd see that the drag had a pretty vigorous timing
behind it, like very slow dancing. That's what it was
too. Smoke Jordan had rhythm in his ears all the time;
sometimes he sang with it, most of the time, in fact;
and sometimes he just walked the floor with it, going
very slowly and barely lifting his feet. You could tell
what it was if you paid any attention, because once in
a while he'd hear fast rhythm and then he could get
across the floor like anything. But he really liked it
slow, and that's what got Gandy mixed up.

When he pushed a broom nothing much came of it;
he had developed a style of sweeping that was good to
listen to, from start to finish. It had its drawbacks,
however, from a utilitarian standpoint; it raised an
awful dust and it didn't get anywhere.

And so he only worked off and on. Gandy fired him
with a regularity which, graphically expressed, would
make a periodic wave. But he rehired him almost as

regularly, because Smoke was almost always around and Gandy's eye almost always fell on him when he wanted something done. He even took a personal interest in him; he tried more than once to teach him to sweep with a utilitarian slant, all the strokes going in the same direction in such a way that when you've gone the length of a room with such strokes you inevitably have a pile of whatever it is, right there in front of your broom, nothing to it, try it.

And then Smoke would try it with Gandy right at his elbow counting for him like a coxswain: stroke, stroke, stroke, forward, forward, forward; no, damn it to hell, not backward; just pull it through the air on the way back so you won't sweep the dirt the wrong direction like I told you not to, you dope. Forward, always forward, like that. But the minute Gandy had to turn away to get the dice box or a cigar for a customer, Smoke would go right back into his off-beat swishing with all the single-mindedness of the unswerving, incorruptible artist.

After Rick came to Gandy's, Smoke knew with the instinct of a compass where his audience was, and he came to sweep almost exclusively behind the bowling alleys where there was no great need of it. And there it was that the black one taught the white one what rhythm is, and not by precept, either. By example. 'Get this,' he'd say before he started a new one. 'And get this. What'd you think of that?' He gave out examples of his work until he had Rick built up to the place where he'd laugh out spontaneously over a new and almost inextricably involved pattern, and after that anything could happen; Rick was a marked man, a lifelong sucker for syncopation.

The thing grew fast. Rick began to sing the songs that Smoke sang; they'd come into his head when Smoke had gone. He'd find himself whistling the tunes, and then the words would begin to spin themselves out automatically, with Smoke's accents and interpretation, as if from under a phonograph needle. Rick had, right off to begin with, a repertory of some fifteen songs that he'd soaked up in the first month of knowing Smoke. They were blues, mostly; somewhat more self-conscious and city-dwelling than the pure-strain, deep-south, negro blues, but born of a common melancholic parent by a younger and possibly white sire. The blues that Smoke, and then Rick, sang —'Memphis Blues,' 'Beale Street Mamma,' 'Stackolee Blues,' 'Wang Wang Blues,' 'St. Louis Blues,' all those — inherited from their elder parent a primitive dignity of phrasing for stories that are eternally the sad stories — poverty, the slow death of love, the awful fact of infidelity, the need to get out and go some place where it will never happen again, to pack your bag and make your getaway. Very sad stories in very sad words that meant no more to Rick Martin than the words of 'In the Sweet Bye-and-Bye,' just so many jugs to carry the tune. The tune was the thing that held Rick to the songs, and what held Smoke was the firm, strict beat, the unfailing four-in-one, that he knew how to send in who knows how many directions.

Smoke revealed himself, finally, for what he was, a professional drummer with amateur standing, and with amateur standing only because he had never been able, what with Gandy firing him so often and the family demands on him when he was in the comparative money, to get himself a union card. There was the further matter of his not having had a bass drum since the time his kid sister, Bluebelle, fell off the sink and went spang through one side of the drum and sort of loosened up the other. It was a peculiar accident; Smoke never did find out exactly what happened. He had the drum down on its side putting adhesive tape on a place that had got scratched almost through; he thought he heard somebody at the front door, so he went and it was Mrs. Johnson, and he just barely let her in when he heard an awful howl from the kitchen, and he ran back and found Bluebelle clean through one side of the drum. Nothing he could do about it; Bluebelle couldn't tell him how it happened because she was too little to talk at the time, and now that she'd learned to talk some she couldn't seem to remember anything about it.

Since that time all Smoke had for a bass drum was a big old suitcase his brother Henry had one time when

he was selling jersey knits. It sounded pretty good
when you kicked it right in the middle, but it was next
to impossible to make the thing stay in one place.
You'd have to keep moving around after it all the time,
because every time you'd kick it, it would move a little
bit. And if you'd set it against the wall it didn't sound
so good; seemed like it needed to be out in the open to
sound deep the way you want it.

Smoke was the first person Rick ever talked to, the
first one he ever had anything to say to. He scarcely
knew his aunt and uncle, and during his library book
period he'd got along without friends. But now here
was Smoke, a coon, no getting around that, with a face
that shone like a nigger's heel, and a mouthful of white,
white teeth that flashed out like so many lighthouses
whenever he opened his mouth, and a clean round skull
covered with close-lying, pencil-width rows of tight
black curls. He was African by nature, too, slow and
easy. He talked more and more to Rick; and Rick,
warmed for the first time by the feeling of being sought
out and showed off for, came back with a few personal
revelations — revelations in kind, about his need to
make of himself a musician of amateur or any other
standing. He told Smoke about the All Souls' fracas
and admitted that he had been on the high-road to
piano virtuosity when the upset came. Smoke gave him
the kind of sympathy he had a right to expect. Since
the trouble he'd had, himself, with Bluebelle and his

bass drum, Smoke's heart went out to anyone forced, like him, to suffer interruptions in his chosen career. He could, of course, play his snare and kick his brother Henry's suitcase, he wasn't quite so bad off as Rick; but on the other hand Rick had a good steady job, he wasn't always getting himself canned, he didn't have to hand over everything he had to his pap every Saturday night, and sooner or later he'd have money enough to buy a piano. No, not a piano, Rick said, a horn of some kind, like a cornet, something you could keep around with you, so you could pick your own time to play it.

'Piano's nice, though,' Smoke said, and Rick, who had been lying awake nights for close to two months thinking how nice a piano is, was the first to agree with him.

'Yes,' Smoke said, 'a piano's mighty pretty when it's played right. Nice slow and nice fast.'

And on this subject — 'speaking of piano' — he brought up the case of his friend Jeff Williams, who played piano in his own band at a place in Vernon called the Cotton Club (and not to be confused with Frank Sebastian's Cotton Club: this one was just a plain cotton club). There were five men in Jeff's band — a tenor sax, a trombone, a trumpet, traps, and a piano — all of them good enough for a medal any place, but, baby, you ought to hear this Jeff Williams. He knew what he was doing. The kind of piano player

Jeff was, the guys in the band tried to keep him playing the piano all night, after the dance was over. Not always, of course; they were all good and they liked to cut loose after hours themselves, but every so often they'd just sit around the piano and listen to Jeff and not give two whoops if he ever quit. And when you get a bunch of fellows, all of them good, that want to put up their horns and listen to another guy play piano all night, you can be pretty sure it isn't just any old piano playing.

Jeff's folks lived just down the street from the Jordans, and it seemed like any time you'd go past there was always some kind of music coming out of the Williams's front door. Jeff was a natural piano player; he just picked it up by himself. He got a piano at a fire sale when he was about twelve years old. They gave him four bits to haul it away and he hauled it home. Pretty good piano, too, after he built a new front and one side for it and got a guy to work it over on the inside. It was still at Williams's; you ought to see it, not a half bad piano, only they had it painted a funny-colored blue right now. It looked much better white the way they had it before, but you know how women are, always wanting to fix the house over, change this, change that. Same way at Jordan's, Smoke said; he and Henry and Nathan and Bud would no sooner get their room fixed up so they knew where they were at and could get comfortable in it than Mrs. Jordan would decide that that would make a better room for Marie and Josephine and Bluebelle, and vice versa, and they'd have to get settled all over again. But it was no skin off Jeff what color his old lady painted the piano; he could play it just as good one color as another.

The more Rick heard, the sadder it made him. He began to think how satisfactory it would be to sleep in the same room with three brothers — all of them good guys — and have three sisters sleeping somewhere in the same house, and a pap to give your money to, and a mother to wake you up for breakfast with the family. And then he'd remember they were just a bunch of coons, but it wouldn't last long; the glow would come back and he'd know, from knowing their boy Smoke, what a fine family the Jordans must be. And then he'd think how it would be to walk past the Williams's and hear music coming out of their front door, and go in and say, 'How are you, Jeff, boy?' and stick around and listen to him play that blue piano until it was time to go home and go to bed with all your brothers and sisters again. The good life, even if they were coons. Much better than peanut butter and crackers by yourself all the time, or a can of spaghetti, even if you were white, and no place to go except to Gandy's to work and practically pray that Smoke would show up and start talking.

It went that way all the time. Rick couldn't think about anything but Smoke in those days; he was

scared to death Smoke would lose interest in him because he really didn't know much to say, himself; he
couldn't tell about his family because he didn't know
anything to tell; he couldn't talk about school because
that was a subject he didn't care to go into; all he could
ever say was that he certainly did want to learn how
to play some kind of a musical instrument. That was
his single point of contact with Smoke, and the only
definite thing he had to say to him. For the rest, he
confined himself to questions that very subtly flattered
Smoke — questions like what did he think of this and
that — and then he listened all-ears while Smoke told
him. It was a nice new thing for Smoke, you don't get
listened to all-ears in a family of seven, not counting
the mother and father. They know all you have to say,
or think they do. Smoke would rather any time go
down to Gandy's — even when he was fired — and
talk to Rick, who looked like high-class white with
new pants and his hair combed with water and his
fingernails clean, and who, despite all this, hung on his
words. Smoke couldn't quite believe it; he came of a
race that isn't used to having its words hung on, and
he kept a wary eye on the line that can't be crossed.
There couldn't be friendship, but there could be talk.

Rick didn't know there was a line. He forgot in no
time at all that there was such a word as coon. His one
concern was to have Smoke like him, or at least bear
with him until he grew up a little and got some ideas of

his own. And in the interim his plan was to spar for time, to keep Smoke with him by hook or crook until the day when he would have something definite to offer him, until he could show him somehow that he, Richard Martin, was as worthy of a friend's respect as, oh, say Jeff Williams, to put it strongly. He felt himself shaping up inside with the conviction that give him time and he was going to be a great guy one way or another — something like a drunk who gets the idea that he's on the point of having the answer to life and death and thought, only he can't quite, at the moment, put it into words, but give him a minute because he's almost got it.

Rick considered ways and means. What he really wanted to do was to hand Smoke his ten dollars — the six one-dollar bills and one two-dollar bill and four fifty-cent pieces that he'd made at Gandy's — and tell him to go get himself a bass drum and pay him back when he liked or not at all, just however he felt about it; but he held off with the sense that between men that kind of thing was pretty fancy, and that it certainly was blessed enough to give, but how would the whole thing make Smoke feel? Like a bum, probably. An offhand, quiet gift would go better, but what? And then the next Saturday night after Gandy paid him he walked home by way of a United Cigar Store — he didn't trust Gandy — and bought two two-bit cigars, and being asked his age, replied that his father, for whom he was doing this purchasing, was about fifty, and it got by fine. He put the two cigars in his hip pocket and walked home with small steps.

Next day he worked until four. Smoke came in about three, sat down behind the bowling alleys, and went into a monologue about how it takes all kinds to make the world. His sister Marie, for instance, got the best report cards in the whole Jordan family(not counting Bluebelle; she wasn't old enough yet). But she couldn't play games worth a damn. She'd never even caught a fly in her whole life; whereas Josephine, who did terrible in her studies, had that very afternoon knocked a pitched ball clean over into the grounds of the bakery and they never did find it. Funny thing.

Sooner or later it was four o'clock and Rick was off duty, through for the day. He had the cigars in his sweater pocket in the back room. He said stick around a minute to Smoke, and then he went back and shoved the cigars into his shirt pocket, closest thing he had to an upper vest pocket, and buttoned up his sweater. No matches, though; that part had slipped his mind entirely until that very minute. Hell, no matches. Then he saw Gandy's coat on a hook. It didn't take two seconds; there must have been five or six in the first pocket he tried, fine big matches with red and blue heads. He took four of them, put them in his pocket, washed his hands and combed his hair, and went out very smooth on the surface to join Smoke. They left Gandy's together without anything being

said about it. Rick pulled Smoke along by the force of
his will, but not far, at that. At the second corner
Smoke said he guessed he'd better be pushing along
home, and that left it up to Rick to pull things together.
'Oh, what's the hurry?' he said in a mush-mouthed
voice he couldn't do anything about; and then fast,
because it was now or never, he stuck out his hand
toward Smoke and said have a cigar, Jordan, with the
accent on the first syllable.

There it was, exposed to the light of a Sunday afternoon, a fine example of a black cigar. It certainly took
Smoke Jordan. He opened his eyes wide to see for sure
and then he said, 'Well, shut me up if it isn't!'

'Go ahead, take it, I got it for you; I've got another
one here for me,' Rick said with the minimum, now, of
savoir-faire. And Smoke rallied, took the bit, so to
speak, in his teeth, and said, 'Anything once.'

They turned, without saying anything about it, into
a side street, and halfway down the block they stopped,
bit the ends off their cigars, and lighted up, each man
for himself. Smoke looked better than Rick with a
cigar in his mouth. Rick's face was too small for it;
he looked all out of proportion; but Smoke was to the
manner born, that one. He rose, full stature; he
attained, on the spot, his majority.

'First full-length cigar I guess I ever smoked,' he
said, taking it out of his mouth and giving himself a
good look at it. 'Mighty white of you, boy.'

Rick let the adjective slide across his consciousness without going deep enough to nick him. He felt too good to let anything bother him. The whole thing was easy and natural now. Smoke hadn't had to admit anything; nobody asked him if it was his first cigar; he just volunteered the information. That was the kind of a guy he was. 'Me, too,' Rick said; 'I haven't smoked since the time I smoked a cigarette I found. I was only a kid then.'

'Did it make you sick?' Smoke asked with real interest.

'No,' said Rick.

'Well, I guess you're just lucky,' Smoke said. And then he told about the time Nathan, when he was a kid around six, picked up part of a cigar and smoked it practically down to a half-inch and he couldn't even get home. He came down the alley by degrees and finally got into the back yard and there collapsed. And he didn't come home for dinner and they were all sitting around pretty well worried, when they thought they heard a cat out in the back yard, but it wasn't, it was Nathan. His mother carried him in and he was so doggoned sick that she didn't even lick him after he got well.

Rick said he guessed the reason he didn't get sick when he smoked the cigarette was that a cigarette isn't so strong as a cigar. Nowhere near so strong. If it had been a cigarette that Nathan had picked up, instead of a cigar, it probably wouldn't have touched him. A cigar's another thing. He tried to do a lot of talking, but after a while he fell silent and just kept walking. He wasn't keeping his cigar in his mouth much now, just holding it in his hand and spitting every four or five steps and then every three or four. He didn't propose, no matter what, to let himself pass out in anybody's back yard like a six-year-old. All right, then, hang on; breathe deep and don't swallow for anything; just keep spitting and hold that fuming thing sort of behind you, and breathe deep and don't for anything swallow because that *would* throw you. Keep your eyes focused too if you know what's good for you. Look hard at something or other. There's a boy.

He kept it up for block after block and finally he knew he had it beat. It was close, though. There was a minute or two in there when he wouldn't have bet a nickel one way or the other; and now that he was out of danger he couldn't remember a thing Smoke had been saying, or whether he'd been saying anything. It takes concentration to put yourself down like that. He realized how close it had been when he saw that they had walked almost to Vernon, over a mile, and that Smoke's cigar was only two inches long. He just let his drop behind him on the sidewalk. No farewell.

After that he felt in pretty good shape, good enough to look Smoke over with comparison in mind. But Smoke was beyond compare, happy as a lark and untouched by weakness of body or spirit, going strong. He might or might not know what Rick had been through, you couldn't tell from his face. He wouldn't be one to say anything about it if he did. He was probably kicking himself for having told about Nathan. That kind of story can be all wrong in its effect.

Rick felt even better when Smoke, with obvious regret, had thrown away the remnant of his cigar. It was twilight and the air was undefiled. 'Where's this Cotton Club place where this Williams plays?' Rick said. 'Let's go see it.'

Smoke stalled. They didn't play Sundays, he said; ordinance against it. Time he was getting home anyhow, he said, let's turn around now. They walked back in silence. The world looked rotten to Rick, and he felt cold around his chest. Finally Smoke said: 'I'll turn off at this corner. Thanks for the cigar, boy.'

Then, for the second time that day, Rick wouldn't be downed. When they got to the corner he said fast: 'Why don't we go down some other night, then, Jordan, and hear this guy play? We could just stay outside and hear how it sounds, couldn't we, and not go in if you don't want to?'

Smoke looked at him solemnly and waited a minute before he answered. Then he said, 'All right, Martin.' And for some reason or other they shook hands before they went their ways, probably the first time either one of them had shaken hands with anybody.

5

ONE thing tends to lead to another, and this case is
no exception. Within a month after the night when
Rick Martin and Smoke Jordan had clasped hands in
friendship over the shared, but not identical, experience
of a first cigar, Rick became an habitué of the Cotton
Club, a back-window customer, but none the less a
customer. Once they got started he and Smoke went
three or four nights a week to stand or sit under the
back window of the Cotton Club and listen to the music
of Jeff Williams and his Four Mutts. These five, none
of them much older than twenty, were so many gold
mines as far as the pure vein of natural music is concerned. They came equipped with their racial heritage
despite the fact that they had been put down in Los
Angeles, of all places, and not, as Nature must have
intended, in New Orleans or Memphis.

Smoke and Rick stayed outside and let the music
come to them, and they didn't strain their ears, either;
anybody could have understood that band three blocks
away. It wasn't that they were loud; it was that they
were so firm about the way they played, no halfway
measures, nothing fuzzy. They knew what they were
getting at, singly and as a group.

It didn't take Rick long to know what they were
getting at, right along with them. He had, himself,
come equipped with the same equipment as Jeff and his

Mutts — the same basic need to make music, the same
sharp ear to discover it. And he discovered a great deal,
there under the window listening to the band — first
time he'd ever really heard a band except for military
ones in occasional parades; opportunities to hear music
weren't presenting themselves on every hand in those
days as they are now; those were the days of crystal
sets for the few. If Rick had grown up in the present
scene he'd probably have had his head perpetually
inside a walnut radio cabinet listening to this one or
that one playing a tea dance. But as it was he had no
chance to be led astray; all he ever heard was the pure
thing put out fresh by the Cotton Club ensemble.

He went through the stages; first he heard the tunes
and they were the whole thing. Those he knew already
he recognized with intense pleasure. Beale Street
Mamma, he'd say to Smoke at the end of the second
bar, and Smoke would say sure enough, as if he'd just had
something pointed out to him. He'd never have been
caught dead saying how'd you guess or any of the bright
things a white connoisseur might have said to a novice.

It took Rick only the minimum time to get out of
this sort of thing, to take the tune for granted and forget it in favor of what was being done for it. They
always did plenty for it at the Cotton Club. The
variations were the real matter, not the theme. What
happened was that Rick, the amateur's apprentice,
sat beside the amateur himself and developed his ear

to ten times normal capacity by the simple process of listening with it. They sat on a couple of upturned boxes, leaned their backs against the very Cotton Club, and listened. Smoke sometimes beat very softly with the flat of his hand against a garbage-can lid that had got out of place somehow; he just held the thing on his lap and let his hands fall against it, and got, as he invariably did whenever he let his hands or feet fall against anything, some very effective effects. He didn't intrude his drumming. He just kept the lid on his lap, so that if he had to do something about it he could. No more than that; you couldn't expect less from so serious a drummer.

Los Angeles weather is all right. Autumn nights stay relatively on the balmy side, and it was no great test of physical courage for Messrs. Jordan and Martin to sit night after night behind the Cotton Club exposed to the Los Angeles elements. It was, as a matter of fact, really very pleasant out there. A beam of light slanted out of the window above them and made a sort of lean-to for them to sit behind. There they could see each other perfectly and smoke cigarettes, not cigars, without having the not-quite-convinced feeling you get from smoking in complete darkness. And yet everything was nicely toned down. For their purpose they were much better off outside than they would have been inside. Inside, the air was enough to befuddle you, and the dancing — the clientèle being mostly negro with a light mixture of Mexicans and Filipinos — was distracting, a whole show in itself. Inseparable as music and dancing fundamentally must be, it is only the layman who prefers to dance to, rather than listen to, really good jazz. Good jazz has so much going on inside it than dancing to it, for anybody who likes the music, is a kind of dissipation. Bach's Brandenburgs would make good dance music, but nobody dances to them; they make too-good dance music. The improvisations of Jeff Williams and his band weren't anybody's Brandenburgs, but they had something in common with them, a kind of hard, finished brilliance.

Smoke and Rick made the walk to the Cotton Club three or four nights a week, after Gandy let Rick go for the night. Good stiff walk too; it must have been a mile and a quarter each way, that makes two miles and a half. They walked down quiet streets lined with two-story frame houses with a date palm apiece in the front yard — reminders that the tree-planting middle class had lived in these houses in another day. They stayed on the streets as long as they could and then sprinted on the stretch up the boulevard. No sidewalks there, and one out of ten cars doing its best to sideswipe them. No car ever got them, though; they both had experience on the business end of bowling alleys.

You could tell that it was the Cotton Club when you got there, if you were any good at guessing and spelling, because the management had spelled it out in alternating blue and red lights across the front of the building, and then one thing and another had worked against some of the most important letters. A good two thirds of the N, for instance, was gone, and the upright line of the L, and the lower curve of the B. Kids with twenty-two's, I suppose, had picked off some of the lights, or maybe cops with pistols and nothing else to do; and a good share of them had gone out, as lights will, of their own accord.

But if the management didn't care to keep up the spelling, certainly nobody else cared whether the blue and red lights spelled anything or not. What mattered to one, and what mattered to all, was whether or not Jeff Williams was in there pitching. The people came to dance, and there was nothing stopping them; some of them came to listen, and they were well rewarded. Smoke and Rick came to learn, and they got proper teaching. They learned the playing style of Jeff's band so well that they should have been known as members-at-large.

This playing style is worth some going into. Jeff's band didn't play from music, though they could all read music. They had two styles of playing, known to the present trade as Memphis style and New Orleans style. The difference between the two is something like the difference between the two styles of chow mein: in one you get the noodles and the sauce served separately, and in the other sauce and noodles are mixed before they are served. Likewise, Memphis style is sometimes called 'take your turn,' and New Orleans has everybody in at the same time. In Memphis the theme is established in the first chorus, and then each man takes a separate crack at a variation on it. This system has the advantage of encouraging competition in virtuosity. It was a point of honor in Jeff's band for each man to get more into his chorus than his predecessor had in his. It made for a terrific heightening of interest on the part of the players themselves, and it left Smoke and Rick, the impartial unseen judges, choking with the excitement of the chase.

But the way they did Memphis was just child's play compared to the way they did New Orleans. Here they were all in on it from start to finish. Each man went his separate and uncharted way, and first thing you know you had two and two equaling at least five. They achieved, you never could say how, a highly involved counterpoint. No accident, either, because they did it on tune after tune, and never the same way twice. Seek out the separate voices and you'd find each one doing nicely, thanks, and then let your ear out to take in the whole, and there it was. It sounds like black magic, three horns and a piano ad-libbing a fugue, and not only that but fugue after fugue, night after night, except Sunday.

The explanation is not simple; it's as hard as a nice

explanation of what a 'sixth sense' is. The only thing you could say is that in this case it was a matter of esprit de corps. Jeff and his band had played together so much and so long that they had developed psychic responses to each other. They were a team using signals that they followed perfectly without even knowing that they had any signals. They knew how things stood from moment to moment in the same way that a pianist's right hand knows what the left's doing. Proper co-ordination established, the thing just goes along.

Rick thought of himself as a pianist, though he hadn't seen a piano close up for three months; and three months before 'Adeste Fideles,' played adagio, had been the pièce de résistance of his entire repertory. When he sat outside with Smoke behind the beam of light, it scarcely ever occurred to him that he couldn't, if opportunity should stick out its forelock at him, go right in there and sit down at the piano and play exactly the way Jeff Williams played. Come to think about it, I believe Rick sort of thought he was Jeff Williams.

It was all very complicated, the way he felt about these things. First there was his absorbing interest in the music, and next there was his deep feeling for Smoke Jordan, the only person in the world he knew and loved. Or it may have been first Smoke and then the music. Whichever came first, the two had to be bracketed together. The one brought him to the other, and the last back to the first. If you poked around you'd probably hear somebody call it a vicious circle. In any event, Rick contrived to go once to the Cotton Club with Smoke, and having broken through as far as that, he contrived it again and again until their going there three or four nights a week became a matter of course. Smoke would come to Gandy's after dinner and hang around until Rick got off, around nine, and then he and Rick would walk out and start down one of those streets in the direction of the Cotton Club. Second block down Rick would pull a pack of cigarettes out of his pocket — the only proof of maturity he had to offer — and hold it out toward Smoke. And when he had taken one himself, they'd stop and one or the other of them would hold a match for both of them. This was ritual, the reaffirmation of comradeship, and they both knew it. Rick took it the hardest. Smoke could always turn to something, but Rick had a special problem always hanging around his neck. Now that he'd forced Smoke to accept him, an unconscious reaction had set in. Nothing could have changed his feeling for Smoke, but he none the less forced himself never to think about himself and Smoke in concrete terms, but just to feel that there they were, he and his best friend, without any descriptive adjectives, just two people, that's all. He kept himself vague about it out of humility, on the one hand, because he knew he didn't come up to Smoke as a man, and out of a kind of vestigial pride, on the other hand, because though he himself would have preferred black to white for his own color at the moment, still he heard generations of his lily-white kind turning over in their graves to tell him he was crazy. The only way out was to do what he did; to hold onto Smoke and never think a thought.

They could have gone inside and watched Jeff and his band at work. Smoke had known Jeff all his life and he had carte blanche at the Cotton Club. Before Rick had come to take up his time he had sat right in the shell with the band a night or two a week instead of staying, as he now did, all the way outside. The thing came out pretty clearly one time when, at the end of one of Jeff's solo choruses, Rick turned to Smoke all excited and said, 'What's this guy look like, anyhow?' Natural enough question; if one of the senses gets stirred up the others have a tendency to claim a part in the excitement. I daresay that not many people ever heard Lily Pons, for instance, hit the high one on a phonograph record without wondering what a woman who sings like that would look like. It's a way the mind has of trying to make the senses co-operate. When Rick turned shining to Smoke and asked what Jeff looked like, Smoke started to answer in the same way: 'Oh, he's a swell-looking guy,' but somehow or other, that's as far as he got. He was going on to say what he really looked like, but think it over, how can a black describe another black to a white? Too many difficult things to deal with. Smoke just said 'Swell' again, and left it up in the air. And Rick saw what had happened and began to talk about the music.

But he got to see Jeff with his own eyes, even so, not so long afterward. He and Smoke usually left their boxes and went home about eleven or eleven-thirty; but one night they lost track of things, and first thing they knew there was the band playing 'Home, Sweet Home' as a one-step with the reed man getting into clear and going absolutely wild on a clarinet. It kept them there until the very end, even longer, until the light at the window above them had flashed off and then on again and the other lights seemed to be getting themselves haphazardly put out, as if whoever was putting things away for the night didn't know exactly which switches to pull. The light at the rear window stayed resolutely on, though, after that first flutter, and then there was the sound of hearty male voices talking and laughing with a kind of helpless happiness, somehow like the voices of track men who break the tape and then keep on running right up to a microphone to say breathily, 'Well, folks, it certainly has been a great afternoon out here.'

Smoke and Rick started back, Smoke saying, 'Doggone, looks like I'm stuck to sleep with Bud, getting home this late.' Last one in, Smoke said, had in honor and in fact to sleep with Bud. And that, he gave Rick to know, was no picnic, no. In the first place he was unadaptable, he slept all pulled up like a baby, and in

the second place he was only six years old and therefore
woke up every morning at dawn feeling funny. No
point in shushing him either. Of course, everybody in the
house heard him, but the one that slept with him had it
right in his ear. Henry, usually, but probably not tonight.

They were almost at the end of the boulevard stretch
when a man ran up very fast from behind them, turned
to look at them as he passed, and then stopped short
and said, 'Hi, boy,' to Smoke. 'Where you been hid-
ing?' He was all out of breath, and while he walked
with them he wiped his face with a handkerchief. Smoke
said he'd been working and didn't get around much any
more. The other fellow seemed to intend to stay with
them, and so Smoke said it — Mr. Davis, meet Mr.
Martin. Davis and Martin looked each other in the eye
across Smoke and said 'Pleased to make your acquaintance' and 'Glad to know you,' respectively. Very
nicely done. Unbelievably well done, at least on Rick's
part. Not everybody comes off looking so manly on the
occasion of a first formal presentation.

The three of them kept together, Davis panting
quite a lot and not getting much said, and Smoke and
Rick pretty blank on their side too; and then Smoke
came through with an explanation.

'This guy,' he said, jerking his head Rick's way,
'works where I do. We been talking about jazz all the
time on the job. Tonight we walked by the club on the
way home to see how you sound.'

And then Rick shoved his pack of cigarettes across Smoke to Davis. 'Cigarette, Davis?' But that didn't do much good because Davis said he didn't smoke, thanks. He just never had happened to get started, mostly on account of his work, he guessed. You can't play a sax and smoke, makes too many things in your mouth.

Rick and Smoke stopped while Smoke held a match for the two of them. Davis got his breath and said straight to Rick, 'Well, how do you think we play?' And this time Rick didn't come off looking so manly; he got a mouthful of cigarette smoke going all wrong and his tongue sort of turned over and he said, 'Wonderful, gee!' But in spite of his vocal and oral difficulties his tone carried such conviction that Davis turned to Smoke and said, 'Why the hell didn't you come in?' in the friendliest way in the world. And Smoke said they just got there about the end and didn't feel like horning in for such a little while.

And that's what did it. Davis said: 'Well, come on back, then. We didn't feel like quitting, so we chipped in and called up for some gin; I'm going to meet Shorty right up here, corner of Adelaide and Boston, and pick it up. He won't deliver to the club no more. You better come on back.'

You could tell he meant it. You could tell he meant Rick too, but just to make it sure he said, 'What do you say, Mr. Martin?' Before he could answer, Smoke

turned to him and said, 'You don't want to get in bad
with your folks, Rick,' very quietly, out of the side of
his mouth.

It was all good stuff, from Rick's point of view. Here
was Davis, the very man who had just done the right
thing by 'Home, Sweet Home' on a clarinet, asking
him to come back, to come right inside and listen to
them play. And on top of that, Smoke calling him by
his first name and not wanting him to get in bad at
home. The two things together set him up so high that
he got back all his poise and said in a good, clear voice,
'Sure I'll go.' And then the social muse put a piece of
showmanship in his mouth and out it came again as if
he said that kind of thing every day: 'But you've got
to let me chip in on the gin.' He didn't have a very clear
notion of what gin was; he was fast in his mind, that's all.

Davis said fine, but not about chipping in, about
coming back. No point in chipping in, he said, because
he already had enough money. And then Rick couldn't
think any more about anything. He just went along
with the fine feeling of having been found acceptable;
drunk as a fiddler before he'd seen any gin.

They stopped at a corner three or four blocks away
from the boulevard and Davis said: 'We must have got
here first. They got a big business these days. Old
Shorty doesn't even get to bed for three straight days
sometimes; on the jump all the time; must be making
terrible money.'

Smoke, who seemed to know a thing or two about these things himself, said: 'Well, I wouldn't want any of it myself. You can't tell from one minute to the next when you'll land up in the hoosegow. How'd it make you feel to wonder whether every guy you peddled to was a stool pigeon or not? Not me, boy; I got to sleep easy at night.'

Davis was thrown into action by Smoke's speech. 'So you'd be scared of a poor old stool pigeon, would you?' he said, and he went into a round of fast shadow-boxing, there under the street lamp, and ended it up by squaring off in front of Smoke and giving him an easy one-two in the pit of the stomach.

'Damn right,' Smoke said, doing some elaborate weaving and slapping Davis a nice open-hand one on the ear.

'Hey you, you big dodo,' Davis said. 'Cut it out slapping my ear.'

'How about you cutting it out punching my gut?' Smoke said.

'How about us fighting this thing out?' Davis said, freezing in an attitude of manly defense, crouched low, both fists up close to his face.

Smoke, with artist's eye, froze in a complementary attitude, and then the two of them, without moving anything but their feet, walked round and round in the circle of light, moving like Apache dancers, holding each other with evil eye and about to pounce. Then they both gave it up at the same time and came back to where Rick stood leaning against the lamp-post.

'Who won?' Davis said, and before Rick could say anything Smoke said, 'He says he thinks I had a little edge,' and held his fists up again.

'Well,' Davis said, 'maybe you did have a little edge. Boy, my old ear feels hot, I want to tell you.'

He fanned his ear with one hand and looked up and down the street, saying: 'Where the hell's that Shorty? I'm going to get you to smack him on the ear for me if he don't get along with that liquor.'

And Shorty, as if forewarned, drove up at that moment on the other side of the street. Davis ran across to the car and Smoke and Rick stayed where they were. Smoke looked solemnly at Rick and said: 'You sure it's all right for you to go back to the club? Sure your folks won't care?'

'I don't have any real folks,' Rick said. 'My aunt and uncle wouldn't know whether I came in or not. It's all right about me. How about you, though; won't yours care?'

Smoke said it wasn't quite the same with him; he'd known these guys all his life and his folks knew their folks and he'd stayed at the club fifty times after the dance and listened to them play, nights like this when they felt like playing. It was old stuff for him, he said, but he just sort of wondered about Rick was why he asked.

Rick was quiet a moment. He'd got hit in the chest with the same feeling he had the day they smoked the cigars and he asked Smoke to take him to hear Jeff play — the feeling of not belonging where you want to belong. His mouth turned way down and then he looked up into Smoke's serious black face and said pointblank, 'Would you druther I wouldn't go?' And Smoke, who wanted him to go in spite of everything, said so, and they put it away then and forgot it. Rick pushed himself away from the lamp-post and poked Smoke a stiff one in the arm, like Davis, and after that they were fine.

Davis, across the street, was standing with one foot on the running-board of the car, talking to the man inside. The motor was running all the time, racing and slowing, as if the driver wanted to be on his way. After a while of it Davis whistled low and gave Smoke and Rick a sign to come over. They did, and Davis opened the door to the back seat for them and said, 'Shorty's going to take us back to the boulevard on account of keeping us waiting so long.' All Rick could tell about Shorty was that he was black. He got inside the car and Smoke and Davis got in after him, leaving Shorty alone in the front seat. Davis pulled the glass stopper out of the square bottle he had in his hand — Shorty's fifths never came sealed; they never came fifths, for that matter, but those were uncritical times in this country — and held it out to Rick, saying, 'Let's have one all around for coming after it.' Rick took the bottle firmly in both hands and tilted it up until he felt the alcohol cold against his lips; then he let some of it come into his mouth and straightened the bottle up fast to keep from getting any more. He was in a tough spot, sitting in the back seat of a bootlegger's car, having two fellows watch him take his maiden drink. He did all right, though; he held it in his mouth, shoved the bottle to Smoke, and then swallowed his mouthful in small, manageable stints. When he finished it up, he held his mouth open to give it air, and by the time he had himself in hand the car had stopped and Smoke and Davis were outside, holding the door open for him. He heard Shorty say a dollar semny-five and then something about a blackbird and a dove that he didn't put together right because he felt too happy to put his mind to anything complicated. His inner tract was warmed from start to finish by his first drink and the knowledge that he was doing, finally, what he wanted to do.

Shorty's car turned down the boulevard going fast in second until they couldn't hear it any more and then Davis said, 'Race you back to the club. The guys probably think I ran out on them, I been gone so long.' And he started off, landing mostly on his heels and making great clomping noises. Smoke passed him in ten yards and Rick wasn't having any trouble; he could have passed both of them the way he felt then, but instead he came alongside of Davis and ran easily, step for step, beside him, because he was feeling friendly and not at all competitive.

When they got to the Cotton Club the front lights were out and the place seemed entirely dark. Smoke, galloping on ahead, went around to the side and turned out of sight behind the building. Davis and Rick went the same way, and Rick stumbled over one of the boxes he and Smoke had been sitting on all evening and almost fell flat.

6

THEY went in. It was a big place with about forty tables and a fair-sized floor in the middle. The chairs were on top of the tables now, the way they always put chairs on tables, one right-side up supporting another upside down; and there was heavy dust in the air. The walls were befouled from top to bottom with murals that showed signs of having been picked up after somebody's local Beaux Arts Ball. It was hard to take them in at a glance, but you were left with the general impression that they had something to do with Hell. Devils, or cuckolds, with tridents figured prominently in Underworld scenes, classic upper-case Underworld, not the thing the newspapers talk about. At the rear of the room was the orchestra shell, very shell-like, fluted along the upper edge, and in it sat four negro boys, one of whom yelled, 'It's about time' when he saw Rick and Smoke and Davis come in. The three of them walked up together, and Davis unbuttoned his coat, drew forth from the inside of his belt the fifth, so-called, of gin, and set it at the feet of a fellow holding a horn.

The four in the shell were glad to see Smoke and made a lot of it. They accused him of this, that, and even of the other, trying to find out why he never came around any more; and Smoke put them off by a system of grinning at the right time. And all the time Rick stood there trying to look unobtrusive, but standing out, just by the force of his contrasting color, like a lighthouse.

There was need of more presentation, and this time Davis did it, very pleasantly and easily: 'Mr. Martin, I'd like you to meet Mr. Hazard ... Mr. Snowden ... Mr. Ward ... and Mr. Williams. Rick smiled at them self-consciously and made his mouth go, but not fast enough to say 'I'm glad to meet you' four separate times. He made an impression on them, though; you could see that. I suppose part of it was that he always looked somehow like a rich kid, very clean and with expensive pants on. He was good-looking, too, on his own hook. He had blond, slightly curly hair and sharp brownish eyes. Brownish, not brown. In terms of color, Rick's eyes were scarcely describable; they had brightness and sharpness more than they had color. They burned like the eyes of the fevered or the fanatical, with a deep, purposeful smoldering that will get out of hand if you don't check it in time.

Rick looked at them one by one, but he let his glance slide right across Jeff Williams. There he was, and he marked him for later inspection. No need to stare at him like a housewife at a movie actor; not right now, at least, full-face and in the presence of all. Lots of time.

Hazard, the trumpet player, picked up the bottle and said what are we waiting for, and handed it to Rick, who said I just had one, and handed it on to Ward, who stood on the other side of him. Nobody, out of deference, I suppose, to Rick, said anything about the three drinks being gone out of the bottle. They handed it around from one to another and each man drank a big one right out of the bottle straight, and then made his remark, usually an expression of mixed pleasure and pain: 'God, that's lousy stuff; I wisht I had a barrel.' When it had gone around except for Smoke and Davis and Rick, the bottle was better than half done and the talk was less constrained. The one that was Jeff Williams jumped down off the platform and stood in front of Smoke and Rick, and said to Smoke, 'You might as well live someplace else, Dan, all I see of you any more.'

'Yeah, I know it,' said Smoke, whose right name appeared to be Dan. 'I been down to Gandy's nights, mostly, and I don't like to take a chance on waking you up coming in in the daytime. A guy works as hard as you needs a little sleep.'

'Forget it,' Jeff said, and looked around uncertainly.

He was, as Smoke had started to say on another occasion, a handsome fellow. He hadn't said the rest of it, either, that Jeff Williams was a rare type, an aquiline-featured negro. Three shades lighter, he could have passed for a Castilian almost anywhere.

He looked now at his men and said, 'Let's be getting at it.' Then he turned to Rick and said, 'Where'd you like to sit?' and Smoke answered for him, 'Put him up by you; he's a pianist.'

Jeff jumped back up on the platform, shoved the piano bench down to the left, and motioned to Rick to sit at the end of it, down by the low notes. Rick jumped up after him, very lightly and with a certain show of athleticism, walked around the bench, and sat down. Jeff turned to him and said, 'I'd just about as soon you weren't a piano player. The way that slug of gin hit me I couldn't say right off which is middle C.'

'Neither could I,' Rick said, 'and I'm not a piano player anyhow; Jordan just said that.' Faced with an actual piano, all Rick's illusions, so carefully nurtured by constant wish-thinking, left him flat.

Jeff looked at him hard, as if to find out for himself whether Rick was or was not a pianist, and then he said to him, 'What shall we play?' And without a second's thought Rick said, 'Play "Tin Roof Blues" the way you do it, you know, when you take the second chorus.'

'It's good, all right,' Jeff said. 'Not everybody likes

it, though.' He clenched his fists tight a couple or three times before he touched the keys. Then he said 'Tin Roof' and banged his heel twice on the floor: one, two, and they were off.

So they played 'Tin Roof Blues,' and there's no way of telling how they played it. You can't say these things; the way to know what happens in music is to hear it, to hear it from the inside out the way Rick heard it that night on the bench beside Jeff Williams.

When it was over, Jeff, still striking chords, said: 'How'd you know how we do that? How'd you know I take the second chorus? I've never seen you in here, that I remember of.'

And Rick said he'd never been inside before, but he always happened to be passing by and he'd got so he knew how they did things.

'You must remember pretty good to know who comes where. I don't hardly know myself.'

'Oh, I don't remember exactly,' Rick answered with that dead ring of sincerity. 'I just get so I can sort of feel when it's coming; I get a feeling that there's going to be a place that needs some piano playing in it; I don't know.'

He broke it off there and gave up trying to say how it was. Jeff turned from the waist and took another look at him. 'You sure you don't play piano?' he said. 'Something about the way you talk sounds like you do.' He said it not suspiciously, but deferentially, as if he felt some kind of force in this mild, white kid, something to be taken seriously.

The bottle was going around again. Ward, the drummer, thrust it at Jeff, and Jeff said 'Go ahead,' and gave it to Rick. And Rick, who was as intuitive as a woman and spontaneously tactful as few women are, took the bottle and tilted it up briefly in sign that he was drinking with them.

'Thanks,' he said to Jeff, and repeated that he really didn't play the piano, that he'd started to try to teach himself and that he was doing all right, but that he didn't have a piano any more. Dead stop, no way to go on.

'Tough,' said Jeff. 'Maybe we could fix you up somehow.'

'Oh, I don't know much about it,' Rick said again. 'I only got started. I wasn't playing jazz, anyhow. It was some other kind of pieces.'

'Classical?' said Jeff. 'I can't see classical for dust. I hear them playing it every once in a while, but I don't know, I just can't see it. "Wrassle of Spring." "Perfect Day." No damn good. The trouble with classical, nobody plays it can keep time. I tried to teach one of those classical fellows how to play jazz once, and I'm telling you he like to drove me crazy. No matter how much I'd tell him he couldn't hold a note and fill it in. No classical players can do it. You might as well not tell them. Hold it one beat, hold it four, they don't give a damn if they hold it at all.'

He meant it. He sat there with the bottle in his hand, talking so seriously that he forgot to drink until Hazard, up front, noticed that the bottle was not progressing evenly and he said, 'Hey, Jeff! What you got in your hand?' And then Jeff jerked up his head and the bottle, drank quickly, and shoved the bottle away from him for anybody to take. Then he remembered himself and turned back to Rick to say:

'Don't get the idea I'm saying you're like that. I didn't mean it that way; I just got to thinking.'

'I wasn't playing classical,' Rick said. 'I was only playing around trying to learn the notes; just practicing by myself. Hell, I wouldn't play classical; I'd play jazz.'

Somebody said, 'Well, are we going to play?' and again Jeff turned to Rick and said 'What'll it be?' and Rick pulled out his second choice: 'Would you wanta play "Dead Man Blues" all together the way you were doing it Saturday night?'

'Dead Man,' said Jeff, and banged his heel down twice, one, two, action suited to word.

Jeff led them to it with four bars in the key, and then the three horns came in together, held lightly to a slim melody by three separate leashes. Then Jeff left the rhythm to the drums, and the piano became the fourth voice, and from then on harmony prevailed in strange coherence, each man improvising wildly on his own and the four of them managing to fit it together and tightly. Feeling ran high, and happy inspiration followed happy inspiration to produce counterpoint that you'd swear somebody had sat down and worked out note by note on nice clean manuscript paper. But nobody had; it came into the heads of four men and out again by way of three horns and one piano.

Rick, at the bass end of the piano, caught the eye of Smoke Jordan, who was squatting on his heels just barely out of the way of George Ward, the drummer. Smoke nodded, a happy nod of confirmation, as one would say, yes, they're good all right; they always were. But Rick only shook his head slowly from side to side in a gesture of abject wonderment which meant to say, how can anybody be so good? What makes it? Then Smoke's face was lost to him, cut off by the cymbal that Ward had just knocked swinging, and he turned his eyes back to Jeff's hands on the black and white keyboard. He played with his wrists high and his fingers curved halfway around, and he pecked at those keys like a chicken going for corn. He flicked each note out clear and fast, and he couldn't have fallen into an empty cadenza if he'd tried. His hands were built to pick, not to ripple, and they inevitably shaped out a style that was torrid, not florid.

Rick watched the hands the way a kitten watches a jumpy reflection on a carpet. And when 'Dead Man' was played out, he pushed his hand across his forehead and said whew, or one of those happy, exhausted sounds. The three instrumentalists up front turned around for approbation from Rick, and got it, not from anything he said, but just from the look on his face. Smoke got up off his heels and then went down again without saying anything. Ward looked at him and said, 'You want to take the drums awhile, Dan?'

Smoke got up fast and said: 'Sure, I don't care. If you want me to, I'd just as soon take them for a while.' And when Ward got up, Smoke was in his chair like a flash and had his foot on the pedal, and began tapping the snare lightly with his forefinger. He looked into the basket of sticks that hung beside Ward's chair, picked a couple, and measured them up automatically. Then he looked with raised eyebrows at Jeff and Jeff said, 'I suppose you want it slow?' 'Well,' Smoke said, 'If it's gonna be good, it must be slow.' And Jeff answered back: 'You hear some of them say it the other way: "If it's gonna be good, it must be fast." Why you like it slow is so you can go into double time any time you feel like it. That's not slow, that's fast.' He turned to Rick and grinned and said: 'That's a fact. He wants everybody else to play slow, so he can play fast. Crazy son of a gun, the only thing in this world he wants to do is tear into double time on a slow piece.' He thought it over and said, 'He holds it slow good too.' Then he turned away from Rick and said to Smoke, 'All right, you stamp it off, yourself, and we'll play "Ida," huh?' And Smoke very willingly beat it out, one, two, with the foot pedal; really slow: one . . . two . . .

The rest of them knew whose turn it was, and they settled down to a low, smooth tune and put their minds to breaking up chords in peculiar, unorthodox harmonies. At every whole note they broke off sharp and let Smoke have it to fill in any way he wanted it, the way vaudeville bands used to play it for tap dancers.

Smoke had the thing under control all the way through. He didn't pay much attention to the snare — he could play a snare any time he wanted to. He played the bass direct with padded sticks and kept it quiet but very clear, a deep washboard rhythm with constantly shifting emphasis. And to vary it further he played the basic beat with the pedal and went into double time on the cymbal, playing one-handed and holding the edge of the cymbal with the other hand to steady it and mute the tone. He was tearing it up so well — and everybody knew it — that the band simply quit for sixteen bars and let him work; and he stayed right there double-timing one-handed on the cymbal and never repeating himself, keeping it sharp and precise and making it break just right for him. He played a drum the way Bill Robinson dances, never at a loss for a new pattern, but always holding it down and keeping it clean.

When it was over, Jeff said, 'Anyhow you didn't go soft while you've been away.' Smoke didn't hear him; he was talking to George Ward, and so Jeff said to Rick, 'If that horse would get off the dime and get him a decent set of traps there wouldn't be a better man in the business.'

'I know,' said Rick.

'But he can't ever seem to get organized,' Jeff went on. 'He's all the time sticking around home playing ball with the kids on the street, or else just hanging around home talking to his folks, or else just hanging around town. He never stays on a job more than a week.'

He sat there hitting chords and scowling at the keyboard while he talked. 'I sure do wish something would get him jarred loose. Every time I hear him play it gets me sort of sore he won't do anything about it. Seems like he won't grow up and get onto himself.'

This was the first time it had ever been given to Rick to know the pleasure of confidential talk, and it had him glowing. He looked at Jeff and made answer; Smoke, he said, at least had music on his mind all the time; he knew that from working with him.

'Then he's working,' Jeff said. 'I didn't know that.'

'Well, not exactly a regular job,' Rick said. 'He helps out at Gandy's where I work. The pool hall.'

Jeff looked at him again and said: 'That must be where I've seen you, I guess. All night I been trying to think where.'

'It's not such a very good job,' Rick said, 'but I'm trying to make enough money to get a trumpet, now I haven't got a piano any more.'

'I don't see why you couldn't use this piano, if you want to,' Jeff said. 'I've got a key to the hall and there's never anybody here in the day. I bet nobody's ever here before five.'

Rick said he couldn't do that and put everybody to such a lot of trouble and everything. But after that he said a thing that he had no intention of saying. He said, 'You don't ever give piano lessons, do you, like a piano teacher?'

The four in front were playing alone, trying things out, and letting Jeff and Rick talk. Ward stood over his drums, watching Smoke play them.

'No,' Jeff said. 'I couldn't teach piano. I taught my brother a thing or two, but he'd have learned it anyhow.'

He stopped a minute, thinking about it and then he said, 'But I guess I could show you some things about it, if you'd like me to.'

'I'd pay whatever you charge,' Rick said in the big way he had.

'I wouldn't want to do that,' Jeff said. 'I couldn't teach you anything, just show you how it goes, if you'd like me to.'

'Well, I'd sure appreciate it,' Rick said. It sounded pretty lame; all the social courtesy had got away from him.

Somebody looked around and Jeff said, 'Play that thing you were just playing again; sounded good.'

And Smoke said a thing that was hard to say; he said, 'Take your drums,' and got up from Ward's chair. 'Don't you want to play them any more?' Ward said, but he said it in a way that cut off all possibility of an affirmative reply. Then Jeff gave them the beat and they played again, and then again and again. Rick stayed right there on the piano bench beside Jeff, but he didn't limit his ear to Jeff's piano; he concentrated more and more on the way Hazard was doing the trumpet work. It may have been the gin; something had him fixed up so that he was playing constantly right up to the place where genius and madness grapple before going their separate ways. It was Hazard's night. Even ten years later, when he knew what he was talking about, Rick said that he'd never afterward heard Hazard himself or anybody else play a horn the way Hazard played that night.

There wasn't much more talk. They played one tune after another. As soon as they'd pull one through to the end, somebody would call out another and they'd be off again. The bottle went around only once more, a very short one for everybody, and Rick only going through the motions. The gin didn't really affect them much; they were young and so healthy that no toxin could bite into them. But it gave them the feeling that they could push out farther than usual, and so they did.

They began to weaken a little when the hall started to turn gray with morning light. When Hazard saw

it he said 'My God,' shook his trumpet, and put it in
the case. The rest of them got up, one after another,
stiff-legged and bewildered. Jeff, folding down the keyboard cover, said, 'Looks like it sort of got late on us.'
Rick looked at him and said, 'It's been,' but he didn't
say what it had been. He very evidently needed a word
that he didn't have with him, and so he only shook his
head in that wondering way he had, and it turned out
to mean the thing he wanted to say.

Hazard and Davis gave the bunch a general good
night and left together, the first out. Then Ward and
Snowden came up to Rick and said good night, and not
only that but come around again some time.

And then there were only the three of them, Smoke,
Jeff, and Rick. They walked out together and stood
by the back door while Jeff locked up. Rick, who was
picking up a feeling for night life faster than you'd
think, said: 'Let's go someplace and have some breakfast before we go home. I don't have to go to work
until one.'

'Can't do it,' Jeff said; 'I got to get me some sleep.'

'How about you?' Rick said to Smoke. And Smoke
tightened his belt with a large, carefree gesture and
said, 'Don't care if I do.'

So they parted company with Jeff Williams, but not
before he and Rick had arranged to meet at the Cotton
Club the next Sunday to talk over problems connected
with playing the piano.

Book Two

Book Two

I COULD put it under a thick lens now, the way they show seeds in the very act and petals curling out in those educational movies. It would be a matter of the voice deepening, muscle toughening, and beard sprouting, phenomena which are of little interest in themselves, and serve only to indicate that the whistling-post of childhood has been whistled for and passed up and that the erstwhile child is now in the clear and going, single-track, full steam, to become one kind of an adult, the best kind or the worst kind or any combination in between.

It was inevitable for Rick to become what he became. Jeff Williams taught him to play the piano; Art Hazard helped him pick out a trumpet when he got the money together, and having gone as far as that, showed him how to play it. The rest of it was a compulsion that kept him tirelessly working. To play the piano, to play the trumpet, to make music. It was with him constantly the way fads are with the rest of us. He couldn't quit playing; it was the way you can feel about solitaire; as soon as you see it won't come out this time you scoop up the cards, shuffle them, and start laying them out again; try it one more time, and if it doesn't come out this time you'll call it off and go to bed. But if you're an old solitaire player, or a new solitaire player, you don't go to bed. You try it again, and again, and if it comes out you wonder if maybe it would come out two times hand running, so you lay them out again just to see. And if it does it would be something of a record three times hand running, and if it doesn't, why it seems sort of a shame to quit when you're beat, so you keep it up until some outside influence like the telephone or simple exhaustion stops you. So with Rick. The fascination of making music was on him like a leech. He'd sit at the Cotton Club piano and practice until his fingernails ached from being sent the wrong way, and he'd play his trumpet until his lip crumpled up on him and shook miserably in the face of further discipline. But he stopped only when he had to, when it was time for him to go to Gandy's or get something to eat.

Or go to school. He got away with truancy for almost eight months, and just when he was beginning to feel easy in his mind about it, Lowell High School caught up with him at Gandy's and raised an awful bowl about him and Gandy both. He had stayed with

his job even after he got his trumpet, because it gave
him two-fifty a week and a chance to see Smoke
Jordan daily without appointment. Those afternoons
of pin-setting, moreover, gave his life something to
turn on, a fair substitute for the routine solidity that
family life usually provides. It gave him something to
get away from and come back to, the tie that makes
freedom valuable. The truancy fellow, I must say,
gave him a tie that was a beauty from this angle. He
hauled Rick into the Juvenile Court, where they made
him wait around for a while to get into a receptive
mental state and then put some questions to him, very
brusque, enough to scare any kid of Rick's constitution
into piety for a good long time. Then they put him on
probation, with twice-a-month reports to make, and
gave him police escort back to school.

And there he was with Lowell High School on him
like an Oregon boot from eight-thirty until three,
Monday through Friday. There were two months to
go in what should have been his first year, and of course
it was a mistake to make him sit there and say 'I don't
know' to every single question they put to him the rest
of the term. Very demoralizing, very hard on the pride.
But sons of the poor aren't sent to the seashore with
private tutors when they fall behind in their studies.
They take their instruction when the State puts it out,
and if they fail they fail. Rick Martin illustrated this
point perfectly. He got to school tardy by eight months

and wholly unprepared, gave out *I don't know* as the answer to all questions, and beyond that was literally dumb.

The Juvenile Court had such a hold on him that he went back to Lowell the next year too, starting from scratch as a freshman. There should have been nothing to it this time; he had an even chance with the new crop of Japanese, but it didn't work out. He'd got his one answer so firmly in mind the year before that it seemed a waste of time to get up any new ones. He gangled at his desk thinking about music and making up long fictions in which he and Smoke and Jeff and Hazard were always turning the musical world completely upside down and smashing their way to triumph after triumph. He could make up six or seven of them in one day, each one nicely timed to last out a class period, or he could make up one whopper, divided into chapters and broadened to get him through the whole day. It was always the same story with slight variations in events. The charm of ever retelling such fiction lay in the author's right, as author, to furnish himself, as hero, with everything he lacked in his non-fictional life. He was rich (at least you ought to see his apartment); he was brilliant (witness his profound critical judgments of music and musicians); he was well thought of by one and all but looked upon as something of a god by his constant friends and colleagues, Jordan, Williams, and Hazard (color deleted, at least not so noticeable); and finally and overwhelmingly, he was what a trumpet player!

He got through the days so, and at three o'clock he was free to dump his books into a locker, get out of the building, and light a cigarette. He might well have been held up to Boy Scouts as an example to support the theory that cigarette smoking dulls the mind and stunts the growth, which was that day's counterpart of to-day's richly advertised notion that cigarette smoking tends to heighten the intellectual stature, steady the nerves, and work wonders for the complexion. And having lighted a cigarette, Rick would go, as fast as he could get there, to the Cotton Club, let himself in with a duplicate key he'd had made from Jeff's, and get started on the Cotton Club baby grand.

There, his day finally started, he worked with an intensity that you don't find in every fifteen-year-old boy; that you don't find, in fact, in anybody but the off-center ones, the ones who have to work whether they like it or not, and not for economic reasons either. Afternoons, vis-à- vis with the Cotton Club baby grand, he shed the husk of indifference that was the protection of Rick Martin, the ten o'clock scholar, and became excited and forceful. He had in his blood the lust to subdue, to force matter to take form. He was more interested in playing the trumpet than the piano, but he would not, for all that, stop playing the piano until he knew he had it where he wanted it. When he had it down, eating out of his hand, he could rest; until that time should come, he practiced.

Jeff gave him pointers on Sunday afternoons. He taught him to play from sheet music, fill in the gaps with proper chord sequences, and elaborate the right hand with more or less conventional breaks — simple things, meant only to give him the feeling. The standard break was not a bad pedagogical idea; if Jeff had reasoned, he doubtless would have said that before you can invent a thing that's really fresh you have to know what's conventional. He didn't reason, but he had a good set of right instincts which accomplished reason's purpose admirably. His trump in teaching, however, was that each Sunday after he got through showing Rick what to do, he himself took over the piano and ended the lesson with a concert that sent Rick off in an ecstasy of high purpose. Sensitive students of music go one of two ways when they hear a really great performance; young violinists, specifically, come away from a Yehudi concert feeling either that they'd better take up tennis or else get more time somehow to practice. Rick was with the last class; when Jeff Williams polished off the lesson by giving him some gratuitous musicianship, Rick took it like the whip of discipline and went away champing with determination. And determination was with him no empty abstraction.

He kept it up. He'd practice about two hours every afternoon at the Cotton Club, and then go home as fast as he could and get something to eat and put in a couple of hours on the trumpet. Then, around nine, he'd meet Smoke at Gandy's and they'd go to hear Jeff's band for a while, inside now, either sitting on the floor at the back of the shell or standing at the back of the hall with the dancers between them and the music. He'd got so used to being with negroes that it no longer bothered him when people gave him funny looks. He'd come to take such glances for granted, as do all those who are stuck with some outward peculiarity. There it is, look at it; everybody else does. The dancers at the Cotton Club didn't try to figure it out; for them he was one of two things, the all-white result of an unorthodox interracial union, or else a white boy of strange taste. The two possibilities flashed fast into their minds and fast out again, and they went on dancing.

Before the year was out Smoke had a regular job playing drums for Jeff. Ward folded up with a stomachache one night, turned the drums over to Smoke, and went home. Three days later he was dead, killed by the poison of a burst appendix.

Rick was practicing at the Cotton Club the next afternoon and Smoke banged at the back door. He said it as soon as Rick let him in: 'Ward's dead.' Rick was miles away; he'd been working hard. 'You mean Ward?' he said when it finally clicked. The two of them stood at the door, Rick looking unintelligent as if he'd just been awakened from a deep sleep, Smoke looking sad.

They stood silent a while, and then Rick's face lost the fuzzy look he got when music was on him, and he came reasonably back into the world.

'Gee!' he said, shoving his hands deep into his pockets and wagging his head back and forth like big business, 'That's going to make it bad. Who'll Jeff get for the traps?' Then the two-plus-two logic added itself up and Rick turned a bright face up to Smoke as if he'd come independently on something very good. 'You,' he said. 'Gee!'

Smoke confirmed the discovery and looked sadder than ever. 'Jeff asked me this morning. Poor guy. Here I been playing his drums two nights and wishing he'd stay sick a little while longer, in a way, or take a good rest for a while, and then he just hauled off last night and died.'

Smoke was maybe going to cry; he kept moving the back of his hand back and forth across his forehead and showed his dusty pink palm. 'Jeff and Davis and I were talking to his old lady this morning,' he said. 'She said he came home that first night he got sick, and after he went to bed he started hollering around and she didn't go in to see him because she thought he was just tight or something, but after while he sounded like he was crying, so she went in and he was rolling around on the floor. She said she thought first maybe he had religion, but then she figured it must be something he ate, so she left and went up to the corner to phone for a doctor, but she didn't know how to work the nickel phone and lost her nickel and started walking. She found a cop finally clear down on Alameda and he phoned for the ambulance, but old George was pretty bad off when they got to him. They had to take him to the county hospital almost to Pasadena, she said, and write up a lot of papers and the next morning they operated on him, but it didn't do him no good anyhow. His appendix bust was what happened.'

Rick turned away to avoid the sight of the pink palm moving so constantly back and forth above Smoke's wide eyes. He walked back to the shell where Ward's drums were, saying, 'Sure too bad.' Then he looked back at Smoke and said, 'When you going to start?'

Smoke, following slowly, said: 'You wouldn't figure a guy all of us knew would haul off and die that way. Everybody knew him. Gives you a kind of a funny feeling for a guy that's always been around like that to die.'

'Yeah,' Rick said, and let it go at that, eyeing the drums.

Smoke, bent on philosophy, discussed death in its narrow aspect and in the large. The large he dealt with very soundly; death comes, he said, to all of us, to the powerful and to the powerless. Take for instance the richest man in the world, he's got to take it on the same basis as a mill hand. It comes one way or it comes another. What's the difference, maybe, how

you die? Or when? In a hundred years who knows whether you got blasted coming out of a trench with an idea of killing some Germans for your country, or whether you sat it out in an electric chair for knifing somebody you really wanted to knife?

'They know all right if you're the Unknown Soldier,' **Rick** said, in defense of an honorable death.

Such incontrovertible tribute to honor broke Smoke's train of thought. He turned back fast to the case in point, to death in the narrow aspect. Here was George Ward dead, and for no reason. Twenty-one years old was all he was. If he could die like that so could anybody, Nathan could, Bud could, you could. A thing like that can make you distrustful, suspicious of the ones you've got the very most faith in. Gives you a morbid feeling about every living thing.

'Old Ward,' he said.

'When you going to start?' Rick said. He didn't have anything to say about death; the only thing he ever had anything to say about was music. From his own point of view as a pianist and trumpet player he could tell you whether a piece was hard or easy; in a larger sense, as critic, he could say right off whether a thing was good or bad. His instinctive taste was infallible within the bounds of his chosen field. Outside of that he was deaf, dumb, blind, even slightly halt and more or less lame. What was death to him; what was plane geometry; what was Spanish Conversation and

Composition? He looked steadily, with appraising eye, at the late George Ward's drums.

'I guess I start regular tonight,' Smoke said. 'I been playing for him three nights, counting part of the night he got sick, and he only died this morning at four o'clock. I don't feel so good about it either. Playing a dead man's drums; I don't know. I feel like I don't know how to play a drum, like I never saw one of the things until right now. I could tell Jeff to get Mort Fricke. He'd do it.'

Rick got a gleam in his eye. First time he'd ever seen anything wrong with Smoke.

'My gosh!' he said with a flash of real anger. 'You mean you might not take the job when Jeff asked you and everything? My gosh, you big horse's tail, something must be wrong with your brains.'

The way he said them they were harsh words. Smoke looked up, shocked; he couldn't believe he'd heard it right. He sank slowly to the piano bench, laid his head on the black and white keys, and began to cry; no noise, but he was crying all right. Rick looked at the ceiling, then at the floor, and finally at Smoke. His tension broke at the sight of the black head bowed in grief for a dead friend and in pain from the words of a live one. He dropped to the bench beside Smoke, threw an arm around his neck, and with his face on the keys close beside Smoke's he made a decent confession:

'I didn't mean to call you a horse's tail, Dan. All I

meant was you're a good man on drums and now Jeff needs one, and you're really good. Why I said it is I like you better than anybody. Damn it, honey, don't cry any more or I'll have to too. I'm sorry I said it, and I didn't mean it. Honest to Christ, I didn't *mean* it.'

He did the best he could, considering that this was the first time he'd ever handled any tenderness directly. His knowledge of the jargon was limited to the lyrics of popular songs. He made it work, though, well enough to make Smoke stop crying. Both of them rose from the piano bench recovered, the one reassured and the other exculpated and neither one embarrassed, though the one had certainly wept like a nervous woman and the other had fallen into the wrong terminology.

Here, Rick said, let's smoke a cigarette. And they did. And after a moment Rick laid his cigarette in a groove above the keyboard where another cigarette had been laid sometime, sat down again, and said, 'What do you think of this?' And he played through the fast part of a piece called 'Dog on the Piano,' a tone poem of a sort, sequel to another one called 'Kitten on the Keys' which was very popular with that day's virtuosi. Rick hit right into it and when he'd finished it Smoke said, 'If I couldn't see it was you I'd know it was Jeff.' The extreme compliment. 'How long you been practicing up on that?' he said.

'Oh, about a week,' Rick said. A lie, a clear-cut lie. He'd spent two hours a day on it for a good three weeks.

'Play that part again,' Smoke said. His eyes had lost their beagle look. The whites were once more white. Rick played again, and halfway through Smoke sat down at Ward's drums, and then it was just a question of time. He and Rick played until the cook was busy in the kitchen and the hall was almost dark. They left together.

'George's mother's getting him up a funeral for to-morrow afternoon,' Smoke said outside. 'You could come if you wanted to; it's just for friends. She asked Jeff to play, and old Jeff don't know what to do. He can't think what to play, because it's got to be — oh, you know how it'd have to be, and he says the piano at the church has got at least six or eight keys on it that won't do nothing but click, and he's scared it won't sound so good. He's going to see if Art will play "The Holy City" and let him just play the piano part soft, if it's all right with Mrs. Ward. It's a pretty good tune. It goes "Jerusalem, Jerusalem." Sounds good on a trumpet.'

Smoke sang 'Jerusalem, Jerusalem' all the way down the block, making his voice ring out clear like a military horn. At the corner where the ways parted he stopped singing and said, 'You coming to the funeral or not?'

Rick couldn't say. It was another one of those questions which, faced one way, require careful considera-tion, and faced the other way, require equally careful consideration. 'What do *you* say?' he said.

Smoke took it slowly. 'Well,' he said, 'it's for his friends, and you're one of his friends; but it will be mostly people you don't know.'

There it was, faced this way and faced that way. 'Oh, I'll think it over,' Rick said with the air of one who doesn't want to do any more facing. Then, shifting his ground, he gave out a question to Smoke: 'You going to play tonight?'

'I guess it's about all I can do,' Smoke answered, and like a good poem, the words meant more than they said.

'I guess I won't come down tonight,' Rick yelled from a half-block away. 'I got some work to do.'

2

RICK let himself into the dark apartment, went immediately to the kitchen cooler, found butter, cheese, and peanut butter. Then he sliced some bread, precisely, and built himself two sandwiches, one of cheese, one of peanut butter, washed the knife, wiped up the crumbs, and taking the sandwiches with him retired to his studio, the storeroom where he slept.

It was as stern a cell as any devout worker could ask for. A naked electric light bulb hung from a tannish braided cord in the exact center of the room, and directly beneath it stood the one piece of furniture, an iron hospital cot. The walls were lightly hung with flaking blue calcimine which did not look its cheeriest in artificial light, but which, on the other hand, did not look it's best in the full light of day either. Rick's personal effects took up one corner of the room. Three pairs of trousers hung by their heels, full length, from a spike driven into the wall, and from another spike there hung two shirts and a sweater. There was an orange packing box, the two-compartment kind, fitted into the corner; on the top of it, diagonally placed, lay a comb, a military hairbrush, a civilian shoebrush, a tin of shoe polish, and a nail file; on the first shelf there was a pile of things, socks, ties, underwear, and handkerchiefs, all laid straight; and on the bottom shelf there was a pile of sheet music weighted down by an oblong, fake-leather trumpet case.

Rick held the two sandwiches in one hand, stood on the cot, and twisted the electric light bulb until the light came on; then he jumped down and went straightway to the lower shelf of the orange box and got his trumpet and his music. He sat cross-legged in the middle of the cot, under the light, and ate his supper while he looked through the sheet music. He narrowed the choice down to two and finally to one, which he propped up against a pillow at the head of the cot. Then he opened the trumpet case, took the trumpet respectfully in hand, and fitted the mouthpiece into place. He held it away from him, in profile, to admire its lines, polite preliminary to the act of making music. This had become tradition with him, and it never changed. He always felt a

mystical relationship between himself and the medium
of his music, a kind of personal, conscious communion,
like love, only surer. It was a sense that whatever he
put into it, it would give him back in equal measure up
to a certain point, and beyond that, anything could
happen; if he did his utmost the horn might even come
back with a bonus, such was the heightened trust between them.

He held it so, in profile, for a good long time, and let
himself be flooded with the knowledge that this was his
trumpet, it was for this that he had set up tenpins at
Gandy's, and therefore had met Daniel Jordan, and had
therefore met Jeffrey Williams, who had taught him
to play the piano, and thereafter had met Arthur
Hazard, who had taught him to play the trumpet.
There in his hand was the silverplated symbol of a
chain of scarcely credible events. He put the symbol
to his mouth, stiffened his lip, and blew a minor blast.
The blast came out the bell-shaped end of the trumpet
and brought with it a tone that it had picked up inside
somewhere. Very satisfactory. In you blow and out it
comes. Blast, blast.

Rick narrowed his eyes and looked hard at the sheet
of music propped up against the pillow. 'Wang Wang
Blues,' one flat. He began to play with a sure, firm
drive, and played it through to the end without one
false move. He put the trumpet in his lap then, pulled
his sleeve across his mouth, and thought it over. Then

he started it again, slower this time and with embellishments, the very embellishments that Art Hazard had written into the score for him to try. It was jerky, and he tried to smooth it out. Then he went on to the second choice in the pile of music, and then the next and then the next. When he got cramped sitting cross-legged on the cot, he would stand up for a while, and when he got tired standing up, he'd sit down in the middle of the cot again.

He went back to 'Wang Wang Blues' finally, and played the bar of triplets that bothered him the first time over and over and over until there came a knocking on the floor above in sign that some fellow man on the floor above was sick to death of the continued triplets or possibly of the whole performance. Rick told time that way. The knocking never came until at least nine-fifteen. He shook the trumpet, removed the mouthpiece, and clipped it into place in the case; then he put the trumpet itself away for the night, tenderly and with regret. Before he returned music and trumpet to the bottom shelf of the orange box, he lay for a time stretched out on his stomach above the music and sang the triplets, quietly and with faultless phrasing, precisely the way he'd been trying for the last fifteen minutes to play them.

He went back to the apartment. Still no one there. He lighted the water-heater and attached the cord to the iron. Embellishment went on apace, but in another field; he pressed his blue bell-bottomed trousers, shined his shoes, bathed, washed his hair, and shaved. He was going to a funeral the next day.

3

RICK arrived at the church somewhat later than the appointed time. He pushed open one of the swinging doors delicately with one hand, while with the other he removed his hat, an old black crusher he'd come on the night before in his uncle's closet, and which he wore for the single purpose of having something to remove in sign of respect. He'd seen hat-holding men in European funeral cortèges in news reels; that much he knew about funerals, and no more.

There was a stirring in the congregation when he entered. He went to the first aisle seat he saw, walking on his toes and holding black crusher respectfully in hand. It was a hard trip, and through it all he kept his eyes completely out of focus in his attempt to see no one, nothing, at all. He sat down alone in a row of seats, cupped his hat over one knee, grasped the brim firmly in both hands and pulled back on it as if he were trying to stop a horse. Then, when he began to feel anonymous again, he eased up and let his eyes come back into focus.

He saw first the bier on which lay the stilled body of George Ward in its gray, flower-hung box. There it was for all to see, a flower-hung box taking the vain stand of protecting that which was beyond protection; and beside it stood a tall black man, a reverend mister, who was taking this occasion, as is the custom of reverend messrs., to evaluate a departed spirit in terms of his earthly deeds.

Rick spotted Smoke sitting in the first row with Hazard and Jeff and Snowden and Davis. He saw only the close-clipped backs of their five heads and the firm set of their shoulders, but in that sight was all sorrow, all solemnity. Five of them, all young, all still on the up-grade, on the positive side, sitting shoulder to shoulder at the last public appearance of one who had been just like them, young and crazy about his work. And now what? There he was, and there they were. Such a juxtaposition gives one to think, or barring that, to feel.

The black reverend did what he could about it; he constructed out of whole cloth and his own head a glamorous picture of life after death, almost enough to make anybody willing to fly to pleasures he has not here, but not quite enough. In spite of talk, the traditional sentiment will prevail among the living. Rick, for one, had no desire to be in George Ward's shoes. And finally, possibly because there was no use talking, the minister's message came to an end, and Jeff and Hazard and Snowden stood up and went to the piano. Jeff apparently had decided that it would be better for the piano to accompany two horns.

The three of them wore dark suits in the cut that was the *dernier cri* of that day: wide-bottomed, narrow-kneed trousers, and jackets with breast-high waistlines — the kind of suit that undiscovered Hollywood extras abandon in Los Angeles pawnshops.

The trumpet and the trombone were on top of the piano. Jimmy Snowden stood by uncertainly for a moment, hunching his shoulders and looking around with the preoccupied air of the self-conscious; then seeing Hazard armed with trumpet and taking his stance, he grabbed the trombone and placed himself so that the bells of the two horns came together at the point of an acute angle. No one in the church heard it, I suppose, except Davis and Smoke and Rick, but Jeff hit his heel twice on the floor, one, two, to start them.

They played the only way they knew how to play, in strict syncopation, but they played softly in deep brass tones, so fluidly blended that they sounded like double stops. Jeff never once came to the front; he felt his way along, didn't trust the piano an inch, and in the end no one would ever have known that there were any keys that clicked on that piano.

They played two choruses of 'The Holy City,' and between them Hazard took the verse as a solo, leaving Jimmy Snowden standing there with nothing to do, like those young leading ladies in the musicals who have to stay in the picture and look like rapture while the star sings his song through twice. But Jimmy hadn't had any training in how to stand gracefully by; he wouldn't look out at the mourners and he wouldn't look at Hazard and he couldn't look behind him, so there was only one direction left and that was toward the gray box. He went, outwardly, through these choices two or three times, and ended up each time looking at the box, seeing it for what it was, and turning away from it with a jerk. The dilemma lasted during the full twenty bars of Hazard's solo, and when they went into the second chorus together Jimmy fell into the music with the natural flip of a fish returned to water. 'Jerusalem, Jerusalem.'

When they had played, Jimmy and Art put the horns on top of the piano, and with Jeff they went back to their places in the first row. The playing had brought them back to everyday things so effectively that when they came down from the platform they looked like musicians leaving the stand between sets, not chief mourners at a funeral.

Rick had been sitting with his ears cocked, listening to the music and trying to figure the intervals. When it was over he looked around to see how the audience had taken it and he couldn't tell much about it, because almost everyone was crying. One woman down in front was crying harder than the others; she was wailing. That one, Rick guessed, would be George Ward's mother. He looked at her to see if she looked like George, but he'd forgotten what George looked like.

And so he tried to figure out which one of them would be Smoke's mother, and again he couldn't form an opinion. For him, Jeff and Smoke and the rest of the band were very separate fellows; each one had his special face, his particular voice and manner, his distinguishing marks, his singleness. But when he looked at the crowd of negro women and tried to pick out, on the basis of family resemblance, the mother of Smoke Jordan, he had nothing to go on. Offhand it was like trying to classify turtles. For one who is no turtle fancier differences don't go beyond differences in size. Mrs. Jordan might have been almost any one of them now forming a line on the right to view, as they say, the remains.

Rick sat where he was. He didn't want to form on the right. He had never seen a dead man and he didn't want to start then. He was not without his normal share of morbid curiosity — in fact he'd been seriously speculating on the problem of whether a negro changes color when he dies — but he had a greater share of squeamishness than is allotted to most male beings, and his stomach in times of stress was hair-trigger. When he saw Smoke coming toward him he knew he was safe.

Smoke said he guessed he'd heard him when he came in, but he didn't want to turn around on account of being right in the front row. Look kind of funny to give a guy a high sign at a funeral.

'That's a good tune Jeff picked, just like you said,' Rick said.

He needed very much to be talking about something, because a woman holding a little girl by the hand was coming up the aisle behind Smoke, and she had the air of being headed toward them on purpose. She was, too. When she came even with Smoke she stopped and said in a low voice:

'Are you going to go on out to the Cimitary with the boys, or would you like to go along out in the car with Mr. and Mizz Rauson? They got room for you if you want to go with us. Me and Bluebelle going along out with them in the car.'

She was a good big woman. Standing beside her Smoke looked narrow to the breaking point. She was wearing a blue woolen coat with a narrow band of yellowish fur around the collar. Her hat was a black satin turban with a single pearl, or mother-of-same, dangling on the front for decoration. She was largesse itself. It was nice the way she talked to Smoke. The little girl kept a firm hold on her hand. She was busy doing her hopping; she hopped around in front of her mother as far as the arm would let her go, and then she hopped in the other direction, around to the back. She was wearing pink cotton half socks and black patent leather Mary-Janes and a white dress with a pink ribbon tied around the middle. She was amazingly tiny and perfect, like a two-day-old black lamb that has just found out how to run and kick and can't do enough of it.

Smoke was ill at ease; he ignored his mother's question and made himself say mamma, this is Rick Martin, my friend that used to work at Gandy's.

The woman had been waiting for it. She smiled a warm white-and-gold smile at Rick and said that she had heard a lot about him from Dan and that, as far as she was concerned, she was glad to set eyes on him finally. Rick blushed from the scalp down and said, 'I'm pleased to meet you.' He was pleased, all right, but he felt his face burning, and so he turned to action. He went down on his heels, saying to Smoke, 'Is this your little sister?' And down there he came eye to eye with Bluebelle Jordan, the old drum breaker, who gave him a shy, white-toothed grin and then hid her face in the hem of her mother's coat.

'Yeah,' said Smoke, 'that's her; she's awful cute when she gets to know you, but she always acts like this with strangers. She won't make up easy.' He went down too and pinched her lightly on the leg and said, 'Where's Bud?' She turned her head very slowly away from the coat until the white of one eye flashed out at her brother; then she said in a very little voice that broke with the start of a laugh, 'He was naughty,' and turned in fast to the coat.

'Why, Bluebelle Jordan!' said the mamma, as firmly as she could at a funeral, 'Bud was not either naughty.'

Bluebelle looked out sidewise just barely long enough to say, 'I know it.'

Smoke said with some pride that Bluebelle was a great kidder; tell you anything, you never could tell whether there was anything to what she said unless she had to laugh right while she was telling it; then you knew there wasn't. He stood up and looked around, pulled back to the reality of the occasion. Rick stood up too. Little groups of people were gathered here and there talking quietly or just standing in the aisles waiting for the last act to begin.

'Gotta go,' Smoke said nervously. 'I'm sposed to be one of the pole bears.'

'Well,' said Mrs. Jordan, 'you want to go along out with the Rausons and Bluebelle and I? I imagine they would just as leave take your little friend out too.' She looked at Rick, making an invitation of it.

'What do you say, Rick?' Smoke asked, neither hot nor cold.

'I don't know,' said Rick. 'What should I do?' He looked miserable with indecision. Smoke's mother took it for loneliness, and was two-thirds right about it. It stirred up her motherhood.

'I know Mr. and Mizz Rauson be pleased to have you go along out with them,' she said. 'You don't need to worry yourself.'

'Well, then,' Rick began, looking at Smoke for approval, 'thank you, I guess I will.'

'You stay with Mamma then,' Smoke said, 'and I'll find you at the car.' He left them, and Rick immediately felt easier. He and Mrs. Jordan and Bluebelle went out to the street, and there he made a lot of fancy dents in the crown of his uncle's hat and put it on, while Mrs. Jordan forced Bluebelle into a sweater she didn't want to be forced into. She set up something of a noise about it, and in the end Mrs. Jordan concluded that the best thing all around would be for them to go get into the car.

'You're the naughty one,' she said, as they started down the street. 'And you saying Bud was naughty. Wait till I tell Bud how naughty *you* were.'

Bluebelle still had tears on her cheeks from the sweater struggle, but she looked up at Rick while her mother was talking and laughed out loud. The mother shook her head and told Rick how it was with her children. They seemed to take turns. Henry, the oldest, was a wild one when he was a youngster. No use trying to do anything with him, you couldn't do it. And then came Daniel, and he was just as easy a boy to manage as you ever saw, stay right around home and mind just like a soldier. She was intending to go right on through them, but Bluebelle, who would have been the climax of the story in any event, climaxed it unaided by looking up at Rick and saying emphatically, 'I'm in the first grade.' Rick took the right tack instinctively: 'How do you like it in the first grade?' 'Oh, fine,' she said, and

she was going to say more, but she couldn't do it. She
had to stop and laugh. She simply couldn't control it.

'Seems like she takes her pleasure out of out-and-out
lyin',' Mrs. Jordan said, by way of apology. 'She only
just started recently; a year ago she was just beginning
to talk. We better get her going to Sunday School
pretty soon now.'

They stopped in front of a blue touring car, a big,
outmoded Cadillac, and Mrs. Jordan said this here's
Rauson's, let's get on in. Rick opened the door for her
and she boosted Bluebelle into the back seat with her
knee, and then followed her in.

'Come on, get in,' she said to Rick, who seemed to be
wavering again. 'Rausons be along soon as all the
boys come out of the church. We might as well be ready.'

Rick got in and sat down. Bluebelle was standing
on the seat backwards and jumping up and down, trying
to see out of the rear window and chanting over and
over, 'We going for a wide, we going for a wide.'

'Set down, now, Bluebelle, and take it easy, can't you,
honey? You been so lively all afternoon I haven't
harly been able to keep my mind on the funeral.' Mrs.
Jordan pushed her turban up an inch or so on her brow,
as if to be at greater ease, as if to relax a bit after the
strain of steering Bluebelle through a funeral. Then
she looked across at Rick and said, 'Was you well ac-
quainted with George Ward, Mr. Martin?'

And that was the beginning of a long, friendly talk

which was interrupted by the arrival of Smoke and the Rausons. Mrs. Jordan herself made the introductions this time. 'This is Mr. Martin,' she said. 'He's a musician like the rest of the boys.' And that seemed to explain everything admirably. The conversation continued uninterrupted except for the final words of the black reverend at the side of George Ward's grave. By the time the Rausons' Cadillac drew up in front of the Jordans' house, Smoke's mother knew everything about Rick that he knew about himself, and one or two things besides. And Rick knew much more about the Jordans than he had ever learned from Smoke. He knew that Mrs. Jordan, *née* Adams, had been the only girl in a family of ten with two sets of twins; that her oldest daughter, Marie, wanted to be a librarian, but that Josephine, the fifteen-year-old one, felt more of a call to be an actress on the stage, a profession of which Mr. Jordan could not bring himself to approve, because he had traveled with a circus when he was a boy.

Rick got out when the Jordans did and thanked the Rausons very much, in those words. Mrs. Jordan, standing on the curb and holding Bluebelle by the hand, said, 'Tell Mr. and Mizz Rauson thank you for the nice auto ride, honey.' And Bluebelle, grown suddenly diffident again, hung her head and said in her littlest voice, 'Thank you for the nice auto.'

The Cadillac drove off, and Rick was en famílie with the Jordans.

'Would you care to come in, Mr. Martin?' the mother asked. And Rick, who had put two or three hurdles behind him that day, elected to slow down. 'Thank you, but I have to go home right away, thank you,' he said.

'Well,' said Mrs. Jordan, 'I have to go in and start dinner before Mr. Jordan gets home, if he ain't already. Good-bye, and I'm glad to have met you.' She started, Bluebelle in hand, up the walk toward the small, worn bungalow.

Rick remembered his hat. He snatched it off and said, 'I'm very glad to have met you, Mrs. Jordan.'

He and Smoke were alone. Without talking it over they began to walk toward the Cotton Club. It was only five o'clock, plenty of time to get in a crack or two at the baby grand before dark, in spite of what he'd said about going right home.

'How'd you get along last night?' Rick said, and Smoke, who could always be trusted to tell you exactly how things were, without any dodges or coloring, said that it went fine, that somehow or other, when he got the sticks in his hand and heard the music there to measure off, there wasn't anything to it; he got interested in playing and couldn't seem to keep on thinking about how George was dead and he had his job. Only one time any of them felt as if anything much had happened, and that was when a couple of the customers came up to the stand and the woman, one that's

around there a lot, said to Jeff: 'What's become of
Georgie these last few nights? Did he run out on you,
or did you fire him?' And Jeff said, 'He hasn't been
feeling so good.' 'That's tough,' this girl said; 'give
him my love when you see him,' and she went back to
the table. It was a kind of a funny thing for Jeff to
say, but after she left he said there's no use in making
the customers get sad; the orchestra business is something like the show business; you keep a smile on your
pan no matter how you feel, just like waiters always
wear tuxedos, and cooks keep their hair out of the way
and their hands clean. It's just part of the job.

'I never would have thought of that,' Rick said in a
voice bound up with awe. 'What do you suppose Jeff's
got that makes him so brainy, anyhow?'

Smoke wouldn't venture to guess what causes brains.
Some do, some don't, was about all there was to say
about it. 'Holy Cow!' he said, leaving the sphere of
contemplation. 'Here comes my other sister, Josephine,
coming down the street.'

She was a half-block away, coming toward them on
the same side of the street. Rick recognized her, but
not by name. He had seen her in the halls at Lowell
and she was in the same study-hall he was in. She had
played the ukulele and sung 'Wabash Blues' at a
Student Body program once, and they encored her
four times, which is pretty good for a black girl in a
mixed high school.

She was wearing a blue middy and a blue box-pleated skirt that reached her ankles, and she was walking in a full, free stride that gave her the look of going to town rather than home from school.

When they came together Josephine said, 'Hi, Danny,' and Smoke said, 'This is Rick Martin.' Rick took his hat off and Josephine said she'd seen him around school. 'Yes, me too,' said Rick, and it was all over; he'd met his third Jordan in one day.

'Why wasn't you at the funeral?' Smoke wanted to know.

Josephine made a fine face, a kind of paradoxical pout with a great measure of satisfaction in it. 'Oh,' she said, 'that girls' counselor, Miss Ellery, got to thinking it over and decided she couldn't do me no favors right at this time. Not only she wouldn't let me out of English last period, but on top of not doing that she picks this day to make me stay two extra periods after school. Imagine! Two!'

'What did you do wrong?' Smoke asked.

'That's what I've been trying to think, too,' said Josephine, guileless as a dove. 'As far as I can remember I didn't do a single thing. The only thing I can figure out is she's got a grudge on me. She gets the worst grudges.'

Even while she said it, her face took on an expression that was very close to Bluebelle's. Bluebelle was in the first grade, and Josephine hadn't done anything wrong, not a single thing, and that, apparently, was the Jordan girls for you.

Josephine looked at Rick and said in a voice of camaraderie, 'You know Miss Ellery, don't you? She's the tall one that wears glasses, not Miss Ellis.'

'No,' said Rick, 'I don't think I do, but I know the boys' counselor pretty well — Mr. Chapman. I've talked to him a lot of times.'

Josephine laughed long and merrily. 'I know them talks, all right,' she said. And then Rick laughed as if he'd meant the thing to be funny all the time. It had never before occurred to him that a talk with Mr. Chapman was anything other than a nerve-wracking business to be sat through half afraid, half ashamed. And here was Josephine Jordan, Smoke's sister, who sat through the same kind of thing all the time and thought nothing of it, even seemed to enjoy it. A great weight fell off his chest; lots of fellows must have Chapman talk to them every day. He'd never got a long view of it before. Chapman became on the spot a generality, and as such he could be looked at and thought about with no awe at all. It changed things. Rick flipped his cigarette into the street, put his hat on the side of his head, and gave Smoke a light tap on the arm and said to Josephine, 'Yah, that old Chapman; I have to laugh every time I think about him.'

They took leave of Josephine and talked about her

all the rest of the way to the Cotton Club. She had stuff, Smoke said; her voice wasn't pretty, one way you heard it, but there was something about it. It ripped out sort of like a horn, and she could sing as high or as low as she wanted to; what she lacked in tone she made up for in range and volume. 'Boy,' Smoke said, 'can she sing loud when she busts loose! When she does the dishes at night we always sort of expect the cops.'

'She was good at school that time all right,' Rick said. 'She was the best one in the whole show. The kids clapped their heads off for her. They clapped so hard that they had to stop the next act while she came back and sang again. Everybody liked her. They had a green spotlight on her.'

They turned the corner and went around to the rear of the Cotton Club. The kitchen door was unlocked and inside, Yoshio, the Japanese second cook, was peeling potatoes like a machine, running a yard of peelings a minute out of the groove of the scraper. 'How you getting along with your work, Joe?' Smoke asked him. The name Yoshio had broken down, as words will, first to Yosho, then to Jojo and finally to Joe.

The second cook did not look up, but he answered in a high sweet voice, 'Working swiftly for making up lost time.' He kept on turning out peelings.

'Where you been?'

'Attending moratorium on George,' Joe answered.

Smoke worked it out and said, 'Funny I didn't see you there.'

'I have not been waiting for opportunity for saying herro after,' Joe said. He was working really hard on the potatoes.

'How far behind are you?' Smoke said.

'Pretty severely behind on time,' said Joe.

Smoke took off his coat. 'Nothing special on my mind,' he said. 'I'll peel you up |some till you get caught up.'

Joe looked pleased but doubtful. 'Impossible to do so,' he said, 'lacking knowledge of method.'

'I don't lack knowledge of method,' Smoke said; 'I'm a potato-peeling fool. I used to have a job working at the White House Café. Gimme a thing.'

Rick stood by looking glum. He wasn't a potato-peeling fool himself, and he always resented anything that was out of line with his own plan of action. Smoke saw it. 'Go on in and get to work,' he said. 'Only work loud so me and Joe can tell how you're getting along.'

Rick didn't wait; he couldn't quite figure Smoke helping the Jap, but everyone to his taste. He folded the keyboard cover up from the keys, sat down on the bench, and thought things over for a moment, wondering what to work on, what he needed most, what would sound best in the kitchen, when could he quit horsing around going to that damn-fool kids' high school and get a job in a band. When are you good enough; how do you know when you're right? He went into one of his fictions: some big-time band leader, Paul Whiteman, like as not, was sitting right out there in the dim hall at one of the tables. Somebody had told him Rick was good and he'd better look him up. So he had, and now Rick was going to play a little something for him, and if he liked it he'd take him on. All Rick had to do was to play, and it had better be good, because old Paul Whiteman didn't come here just because he didn't have anything else to do. His pianist had just died of appendicitis, see, and he was stuck without anybody good enough to take his place. Play, boy, play.

All right, Mr. Whiteman, how does this strike you? Rick pushed his hat to the back of his head, sat up very straight, like Jeff, and hit into a piece called 'The Sheik,' which was so new that even the Cotton Club band hadn't got around to working it up yet. Scoop. Rick had heard it twice on a record at Woolworth's and looked carefully at the sheet music on display at Silverman's Music Store. He went straight through it, no trouble at all; the second time it went even better, and the third time around he really made something of it. This was the first time he had ever done any impromptu work, and it went so well that he forgot Mr. Whiteman completely and yelled out to Smoke in the kitchen, 'What do you think of that?'

Smoke came into the hall drying his hands on a flour sack. 'What's the name of that?' he said. 'Seems like I've heard it before. It feels like I've sort of been hearing it around the corner like, for a week or so, but I don't ever seem to catch right up with it.'

'"The Sheik,"' said Rick, only he called it the 'Shike,' never having heard it said, and not even knowing what one was.

'You're getting to be damn near as smart as Jeff,' said Smoke, wide open with admiration, 'getting onto new stuff before anybody hardly knows about it; just springing it out of a clear sky.'

'Aw, hell,' Rick said, pleased stiff and blushing.

'Play some more of that,' Smoke said, and Rick obliged him with all the good will in the world. He obliged him again and again and again. He no longer had any reason for the hanging back that passes for modesty. The afternoons of practice after school and the Sunday meetings with Jeff were finally bearing the kind of fruit that is the natural consequence of constant cultivation. Two years now since the afternoon he'd stopped in at All Souls' Mission and started wondering about how to play the piano. And now he didn't need to wonder any longer. He knew. Out of so much cause had come an effect. His head and his hands were working together. He could play now, well enough to become the kind of pianist he wanted to be. The ground was laid, and he was free to devote himself to the details that make the difference between one thing and another.

'You're getting good,' Smoke said. 'I mean good enough to get you a job somewheres playing.'

Rick took his hands off the keys and rolled his eyes around, bewildered. 'If I quit school now,' he said, 'they'd throw me in the reform school or jail or something. I've still got to go to court the first Saturday of every month and let them bawl me out for not doing good in my studies. I don't know *what* they want. I go to school every damn day of the week and still they aren't satisfied. Once you get in wrong they hound you to death.'

'Whyn't you try to get a job playing nights and go to school days? Old Jeff did that. You only got two more years?'

'Oh, hell no,' Rick said. 'I'm only a freshman, and I probably will be another freshman next year too, if they take it in their head not to pass me. I don't know what I'd better do; I've only been late just once all this month, and today for the funeral was the only time I've quit early since before Christmas. It's just like your sister said; they take it in their head to have a grudge on you, you might as well give up.'

'Tough,' said Smoke.

'And there's another thing, too,' Rick said. 'I sort of want to get so I can play the trumpet better before I try to get a job. I'd rather play a trumpet than a piano — I don't know, seems like it's closer up to your head somehow. You play a piano you play it way down here, but with a trumpet you put it right up beside you on your mouth and it feels like you got more to do with it. I don't know — it's just sort of the way I feel, I guess.'

'I never thought of that,' Smoke said. 'Sounds like they might be something to it, the way you say it.'

Book Three

Book Three

~~~~~~

1

THE summer Rick Martin was twenty he was playing
first trumpet for Jack Stuart and His Collegians at the
Rendez-Vous Ballroom in Balboa, thirty miles down
the coast from Los Angeles. 'Collegians' was no idle
boast: Jack Stuart himself was a collegian from way
back; he had attended the University of Oregon on
three separate occasions. The second trumpet was a
bona fide third-year music student at Berkeley, and
the drummer had gone to U.S.C. for one semester.
These three made up the college contingent of the
Collegians; the other seven were college age, and that
was as far as it went.

They had a good band, and from the first week on,
Rick was the power behind it. In any band worth
talking about, some single musician gives spark to the
crowd, keeps them from resting easy, gives them something to shoot at. Even in a band like Jeff's where you'd
be hard put to it to pick the best musician, the same

thing happens. Straight musicianship being at a parity, the men look to the one of them who has the vision, the real sense of things — Jeff, in that case. And in this case, Rick.

Jack Stuart got Rick from the Hawaiian Gardens in Ocean Park, where he'd been stuck for almost a year in an outfit that featured an Hawaiian trio. A misplaced sense of pity and loyalty kept him there doing his best to whip the broken-down trombone man into shape to team with him in Hazard-Snowden style. It was no good. The trombone man was too far gone to be any longer willing to get into shape, and Rick stayed on mostly because he didn't know how to quit. Then somebody in the union put Stuart on his trail and the problem solved itself.·

The Collegians' engagement was for eleven weeks and the pay was fifty dollars a week. They went down the last week in May to start rehearsals and get established.

Rick made the trip alone on the Pacific Electric train and arrived in the center of what business district there was at ten o'clock on a Monday morning. It was his first trip south of Long Beach. He got off the car, set his suitcase and his trumpet case down in the sand beside the tracks, and after the train had gone he just stood there feeling the warmth of the spring sun and smelling the salt and hearing the breakers. It was the first time he'd ever stopped to notice these things.

You don't feel the touch of nature around Central Avenue in Los Angeles, and Ocean Park, as Rick knew it, has perverted what natural flavor it might once have had. There he could not see the sea for the roller coasters. But Balboa is something else. It is a peninsula about five miles long and a half mile across, so that on one side there is the open sea rolling up breakers six feet high, and on the other side there is a placid lagoon that is widened and deepened at the upper end to form a yacht basin. Compared to the beaches around Los Angeles, this one is Cape Cod itself. It is a base for deep-sea fishermen, but there are no canneries to clutter things up. And no roller coasters and no kewpie dolls.

Rick stood beside the tracks at the main intersection of the town. All four corners were built up. On one there was a bank; across the street from it a real-estate office; and the other two corners were held down by a restaurant and by a building that was even then in the process of being labeled the RENDEZ–VO —. The painter had the U and the S blocked out, but he had stopped to sit down on the scaffold and smoke a cigarette before getting the last of the painting done. Below the scaffold, leaning against the building, there was another sign, painted on canvas and torn in a couple of places. The lettering was done in mock-Chinese script — The Green Dragon — and the dragon himself was right there sliding in and out between letters. The place was evidently being rechristened.

Rick picked up his suitcase and his trumpet case and crossed the street. The narrow side of the Rendez-Vous was a soda fountain with a counter open to the street and stools on the sidewalk. Rick sat down on one of the stools, and when he felt the sun go through his coat and hit him between the shoulder blades, he yawned and took off his hat.

A man with a white apron and a white overseas cap came through a door at the back, set a glass of water on the counter in front of Rick, and asked him what it would be. 'Double straight coke with a lot of ice,' Rick said. 'Lot of ice,' echoed the man behind the counter, as if it were rush hour and he was breaking his neck to keep his orders straight.

'Anybody in this town but you and me and the painter?' Rick asked. The sun was warm and the air was salty and everything was fine, but what becomes of a dance band if nobody comes to dance?

The man behind the counter said maybe not this week, but come back next week if he wanted to see a mob. All a matter of school getting out. One week nobody and the next week college kids till hell wouldn't have them. He talked man to man with Rick without making the mistake of assuming that he might be a college boy himself. You wouldn't have made that mistake about Rick at twenty. He dressed like a college boy, his hands were clean, and there was nothing much wrong with the way he talked, but there was something

in his face that marked him as no college boy. It was
the tight, nervous face of a man who knows something,
the kind of face that goes with passion of whatever
sort. You see it in revolutionaries, maniacs, artists —
in anyone who knows he will love one thing, for good
or ill, until he dies.

'They're fixing up the dance floor in there now,' the
man behind the counter said. 'Last summer, or I guess
it must have started summer before last, the college
crowd started to come down here, and it boomed the
town, in one way. Some big real-estate man from Los
bought this place. He's changing the name and making
the hall bigger, and I understand he's getting a different
orchestra, fixing up for a heavy season.'

Rick had finished his drink and was blowing ice
neatly out of his mouth and making it bounce into
the gutter across the sidewalk. He was so full of the
good feeling of leisure that comes just before an auspi-
cious starting to work that he didn't even ask the man
about a place to live. He just sat there and blew pieces
of ice out of his mouth and watched them bounce, and
didn't care whether he walked up the street to the
beach or down the street to the bay, or stayed where he
was. And before he got around to deciding, four men,
one of them Jack Stuart, turned the corner, and the
leisure was gone.

Jack Stuart had an extra-curricular collegiate look
to him, no doubt about that; he was wearing white

linen knickers — plus sixes or possibly plus eights — and a white shirt open at the neck, and, pinned to the front of it, an outsize fraternity pin with more pearls than you'd care to count. He had black curly hair and a genial, man-of-the-world manner. He stuck out his hand to Rick, gave him a handclasp so firm that it hurt, and said, 'Glad to see you, fella; meet some of the rest of the crowd.' Rick met them, and at the end he knew precisely which was which: in the order of their presentation they were drums, saxophone, and trombone.

'Have you got it with you?' Stuart said at the end of all the handclasping, and Rick said, 'Yes,' and pointed to his trumpet case on the stool beside him. 'When do we start?'

Stuart laughed and said: 'Take it easy. We don't start until Saturday night. Let's go in and look things over.'

The five of them walked up the steep incline to the double doors and went inside. It was a very long and narrow hall, and at the far end there were three men down on their hands and knees sanding and scraping the floor. There was a grand piano on the stand and a lot of chairs. Jack Stuart said, 'It looks as if they've already got this front part waxed.' He took a short run and slid twenty feet or so down the floor. Rick jumped up on the stand, put his trumpet case on the piano bench, and started setting chairs together the

way they should go, in threes: reed section, brass
section, rhythm section, and the extras one on top of
another in a corner. Sliding on a floor wasn't his line.
He pushed the trumpet case over, sat down on the
bench, and began to hit chords to see how the piano
was, and after that it wasn't long until he was playing,
and not much longer until he was playing the hard way,
really trying things. It brought the collegians right up
to him, hanging on the piano, looking the new man over.
He was supposed to be a trumpet player.

When Rick stopped playing, Jack said, 'You certainly play whorehouse piano, fella, and nigger whorehouse at that,' leaving it up in the air whether or not
he meant it to be a compliment. And when Rick blushed
in the unmistakable way he did, Jack laughed loud and
long and said he guessed he'd sized things up better
than he thought, by the color of Martin's face. He
pushed in beside Rick on the bench, saying, 'Forgive
me, brother; let's play four hands.' Rick had the bass
end; he gave out some chords in A flat and Jack played
'Yes Sir, That's My Baby.'

He didn't have Rick's ability to strike into the deep
levels of a piano's subconscious, but he was all right.
He played about the way most American boys do when
they have behind them a natural feeling for music and
on top of that a history of an hour-a-day's practice
firmly supervised by some disciplinarian in the family.
It usually happens with this kind of boy that at the

age of sixteen when he's interested in dancing and popular music and general social accomplishment he suddenly finds out that he can play, that the years of practicing an hour a day have brought him to the place where he can read sheet music or even work up popular tunes by ear. So he gets a revival of interest in playing the piano, and sometimes he keeps it up and, like Jack Stuart, makes a business of it. Jack was, you could tell from one chorus of 'Yes Sir, That's My Baby,' a competent pianist.

Rick moved off the bench, set his trumpet on a chair, and let Jack take over the whole piano. And while Jack played, Rick looked the trombone man over with speculative eye, trying to find some outward indication of what he might be worth. He seemed not so slick as the other three; he missed being a fat boy by about twelve pounds, and he had a round, candid face that might indicate stupidity or earnestness or some of each. He was standing a little bit away from the piano, so Rick went up to him and began his ground-clearing. No harm in finding out what the brass in this band was going to amount to.

'Who do you think is the best trombone player in the country?' Rick asked him, straight out, like a kid saying to another one, 'Where's your old man work?'

It was as good a way as another to approach this boy. He thought a moment and said, 'Playing now? I think Jack Teagarden.'

'Uh-huh,' said Rick solemnly. It was one of the right answers, but it didn't reveal a prying mind. It left him feeling that the thing had been resolved too easily — as if you asked someone who's his favorite writer. 'Living now?' he asks. 'No,' you say, 'any time.' And quick as a flash he gives his answer: Shakespeare. It's an answer you couldn't quarrel with, but it might have seemed more satisfactory, since he had at his disposal all the writers of all time, if he'd spent more time looking the ground over. If he'd said, for instance, that La Fontaine, across the channel, or Racine weren't to be overlooked, or that there's something to be said for Milton, and then had gone ahead and chosen Shakespeare, it would have meant more.

'Have you heard this boy Snowden that plays trombone for Jeff Williams?' Rick asked him.

'Oh,' the boy said, 'niggers. I was thinking about white bands. Niggers are in a class by themselves.'

Now they were getting somewhere. Rick looked at the boy and said: 'That's a funny thing. You'd think any white man could learn to play as well as a negro.' He paused and thought it over, and then went on in a voice of a peculiarly different quality: 'Well, I think a white man could do it, all right, if he'd only try hard enough to. But these negroes don't even seem to have to try; they're just born that way. You say you'd heard this boy Snowden?'

'Just records,' the boy said. 'You hear a lot about

Williams's band, but they never seem to be playing anywhere where you can hear them.'

'They've been mostly in Chicago and New York the last three years,' Rick said, 'but I've got every record they ever made. First one was "Dead Man Blues" with one of Williams's own pieces, "Black Scramble," on the other side. Didn't you ever notice Snowden's chorus on "Black Scramble"?'

'I can't say I have,' the boy said; 'it must have been a pretty long time ago.'

'If you'd ever heard it, you'd know,' Rick said. 'It's the — oh, I don't know, it's not like anything you ever heard tell of. It doesn't even sound like a trombone much, the way Snowden plays that chorus. The way he plays it, it sounds more like a trumpet, everything sharp and not gliding. He doesn't play a valve trombone either, just a regular slip-horn. You don't see how he does it.'

'What are you fellas saying about me?' Jack said, looking up from the piano keys, very well pleased with things.

'Nothing. This guy,' the trombonist said, pointing a thumb at Rick, 'says he's got every record Jeff Williams's band ever made.'

'That so?' Jack said. He stopped playing. 'Why didn't you bring them along?'

'I did,' Rick said. 'They're right here in my suitcase, all fourteen. I've got them here but I haven't got a phonograph. You can usually find a phonograph, though.'

'Bob Jones the second trumpet's got a portable with him. Up at the house. We've been taking it down to the beach in the afternoons.'

'I don't want to bust any of these records,' Rick said. 'A lot of them you can't get hold of any more since Williams got popular.'

He spoke in the tone of a connoisseur, a trusted keeper of the seal, and the collegians seemed disinclined to take exception to his stand.

'You must think Williams is pretty good,' was all that Stuart said.

'Yes,' Rick said, 'I think he's the best.'

They took that, too, from him. Something about the way he said it gave it an edge, made it incontrovertible, and more than that, convincing.

They stood around the piano, quiet, all of them looking at Rick, and finally Jack Stuart got up from the piano and said, 'Let's go; I'd like to finish my tan this week without burning all the hide off of me.'

'Get some of that E.Z. Tan dope,' the drummer said. 'I got a peachie tan last summer with that.'

'No, thanks,' Jack said. 'I'm the kind of a man that can't stand any greasy stuff on me. The only way to get a tan is to go out about an hour a day the first week and keep zinc ointment on your nose.'

The first week went that way. They had a house

together on the bay front, five bedrooms for the ten of them and a living-room, dining-room, and sun porch. They took their meals at the restaurant across from the Rendez-Vous and used their own kitchen as a workshop in which they worked all possible combinations of bootleg gin and mixers, orange juice, lemon juice, grapefruit juice, grape juice, ginger ale, lime rickey, coca cola, and on one occasion root beer.

They got up late, all the way from eleven until one; they lay around on the beach all afternoon, interpolating periods of athleticism when they put on shoes and kicked a football up and down the beach, or played Sink the Ship, or rode breakers. All ten of them got fierce sunburns. Rick's was so bad that he was delirious all one night and got blisters that he could roll very carefully from his elbows to his shoulders just by raising and lowering his arms. Very bad blisters. It was a rotten start. It was impossible to get all ten of them in a mood to rehearse at the same time. If the leader had been tougher, he might have kept them in some kind of order and got them down to work, but Jack Stuart was first of all a collegian, and with him the going was always easy. And that first week was more like a fraternity house-party, stag and unfettered, than anything else.

The round-faced trombonist, Eddie Phelps, shared a room with Rick. He was more tractable and less volatile than the others, and Rick fed him Snowden choruses, one after the other, until he built up his taste for them. It was Phelps's first good job, and he meant business; he was willing to be taught anything, and Rick was willing to do the teaching. The two of them left the beach and went back to the house every day at about three and tried things out, sitting in the sun porch in their bathing suits. When the rest of the crowd came in around six, there they'd be, glistening with sunburn salve, sitting on the edges of a couple of wicker chairs and blowing out good brass duets one after another. It put the rest of them in a mood to play, as a rule, and all ten of them would play around for a half hour or so, fighting for solos and finally breaking off one by one to go mix a drink and get dressed for dinner.

Two nights before the opening they had a systematic rehearsal at the Rendez-Vous. They took the instruments, lights, and stands and a gallon of gin down to the hall before dinner and left them there all ready to go. They were all serious and intent during dinner, and when they went back to the hall and began tuning and shoving chairs around, there had developed a real excitement, something like the spirit that gets into a football squad after the first string has been picked and they're in the gymnasium ready and waiting for a pep talk from the coach before serious practice begins. It's a good sort of hysteria, and too bad it always gets put to wrong uses like athletics and militarism. It was working fine on this crowd; after a full week of the most

unregenerate playing around and downright slothful-
ness, here they were, Jack Stuart's ten collegians, all
primed to become overnight the greatest band in the
world. Ready and willing.

Jack had arrangements of eight new tunes still in the
publisher's box unopened. He ripped the box open with
a pen knife and started calling them off: trombone,
first trumpet, second trumpet, piano (that's me), bass,
first sax, second sax, third sax, guitar — over and over
until all the music was given out.

'Now keep these straight,' Jack said; 'I'm not
responsible for any guy losing his music. These are
damned good arrangements, too, at least they ought
to be for what they cost me.'

He stood up. He was handsome in a way that didn't
mean anything. He had the empty, regular face that
you can find ten to a row in college courses called
Economics 10B or Political Science 101, or the sort of
face you see on young leading men in the second feature
of moving-picture double bills. He was the showman of
the band, and he would be even better at it when his
tan got established and his cheeks and forehead stopped
peeling and flaking off. Right now the face was clouded
with authority. Straw boss over ten musicians.

'First of all,' he said, and he cleared his throat to
give weight to his words, 'first of all I want you to
remember that we're a dance orchestra and our first
job is to play a tempo that they can dance to. And it

must be smooth. And another thing, this is a high-class place, all-college crowd. They aren't going to allow any gobs on the floor at all. So you see what that means?'

The straw boss was liking this, warming right up to it. Who was the brains of this outfit; who knew how to figure this kind of thing out? Jack Stuart, that's who.

'What it means is that we're playing to our own kind of a crowd, and we won't be playing one-steps for a bunch of snaky Jews and department-store girls. It will be mostly frat men and sorority girls down here, and the main thing we want to do is introduce the Charleston and put it over. It's the rage now in the East, and if we can be the first to get it started on this coast, we're made. The manager has got a guy from Hollywood that's going to be here all summer giving lessons in the afternoon. That ought to get things going.'

The boys were all in their places listening to it, nodding their heads at the big-business phrases. Rick listened as respectfully as any of them, but he kept an eye on his stack of music and kept shifting it around until he'd got a look at most of the first trumpet solos. He got a look at the notes and heard them in his head the way he'd play them, and he was doubtful. His face took on the sceptical look with which wary young ones will look at a glass of milk or a portion of cauliflower: simple distrust with a germ of rebellion.

As soon as Jack stopped talking Rick said, 'Are these eight tunes all we're going to play?' And Jack said no, he had some more coming, but what did he want for a nickel anyway? Eight tunes, all of them brand new, just off the press, ought to hold any band for one rehearsal. Hardly anyone had heard these pieces at all. That one called 'Ah Ha!' for instance was going to make the best novelty number anybody ever heard. Room for a lot of clowning in that one. Nothing in the world will set a band up like a lot of good novelty stuff.

Rick listened, and then he said, 'Are we supposed to play these as written all the way through, every time the same way?'

'Sure,' Jack said. 'What's wrong with them? They're the best arrangements money will buy. What do you want, anyhow?'

Rick looked sad. 'Maybe they're all right,' he said. 'Maybe they'll sound better than they look, but look at this number six.'

Jack went over to Rick's stand and looked. Rick pointed to the page and said, 'See how it goes?' He sang it off, and then took up his trumpet and played it. 'It's all right,' he said, 'in a way; but you wouldn't be able to play that that way every time. That's why I asked; do we get to play our own solos or do we just play the written ones? This is so sort of — oh, I don't know — it's not — it's sort of what you'd expect.'

Jack was sore. He looked down his nose at the score

and said in as cold a voice as he could manage: 'All right, you're such a ball of fire, improve on it, if you're so good. But get this straight; this isn't any coon band like this Williams' you're always yapping about, and I don't want it to sound like one. We're playing for a refined crowd.'

He walked off and Rick said to his back, 'I just wanted to know.' And Jack, looking straight ahead of him, said, 'Now you do, I hope.'

And so, during the rehearsal Rick gave the arrangements their chance. He played exactly as written, and he played so well, took his solos with such restraint and such beautiful phrasing and feeling that before ten o'clock Jack was out of it and looking on him with definite approval. Rick was easily the best musician in the band; Jack could see it, anybody could have seen it.

When they knocked off at ten to have a drink after having gone through number six three times for the benefit of the reed section, which was having a time with the problem of solidarity, Jack walked up to Rick, touched lily cups with him and said: 'Here's to a big season, fella. It looks good from here.' And Rick repeated 'Big season' and drank it down.

They were apart from the others and Jack said, 'What do you think of Jones?' — the second trumpet. 'I think he'll be all right,' Rick said. 'He's just a little anxious or something, and I think he's playing with the beginning of a roll.'

'How do you mean roll?'

And Rick with pedagogical thoroughness explained what a roll is. It's a habit, and a ruinous one. He heard this boy Jones playing a little sharp on high notes, and so he took a look at him and there it was — a roll — not bad yet, but on the way. It comes from dropping the mouthpiece too low on the lower lip, and if you keep on playing that way you get so you can't bring it up where it belongs; somehow you just can't do it. It's the hell on trumpet players, he went on to say in the same tone people use when they talk about incurable diseases.

'The way a fellow explained it to me,' he said, 'was that a rolled lower lip is like a nozzle on a hose. Say your lips are a hose; if you close the nozzle, the water, which is your air, in comparison, see, backs up or swells up in the back of the hose, which is really your throat, see? When you open up the nozzle of a hose the water flows out easy, comes right out, same rate of speed all the time.' He had his forehead puckered up with lines going in three directions, he was trying so hard to keep the figure straight.

'It's like this,' he went on, though Jack was obviously wanting to get on with his drinking and stop having things explained to him analogically, 'you get a roll and it closes up your lips and gives you a choked feeling in your throat, and you get tireder than Christ himself after about a half hour of steady playing.

That's what puts so many brassmen in the nut house, and I mean it. They blow their heads off and get dizzy and if they keep it up they're dizzy all the time. The only way to play good is to take your horn and your breathing for granted; then you can think about how you want it to be; you just think it and it blows right out the other end of the horn. You know,' he said to Jack, who by that time was on one foot and then the other so fast it began to look like a dance, 'you know, when I was first starting in to play trumpet, I was sort of teaching myself, practicing on stuff I'd hear other fellows play, and without knowing anything about it I was beginning to develop a roll. One day I was showing this fellow that gave me lessons once in a while, I was playing something for him to ask his advice about it, and I just barely put the horn up to my mouth, and he let a yell out of him like he'd seen a spook. "God Almighty, boy," he said, "you're getting a roll there like a tramp!" I didn't even know what one was.'

'Is that so?' said Jack. 'Let's go over and have another drink.' They went to the jug and Rick kept the narrative going. 'Well, this fellow told me to quit playing trumpet for a while until I got the idea out of my head, and all that week I just went around holding my mouth the way he said to, with my lower lip tight against my teeth, and no higher or lower; the way Art told me to do it was to figure it was just

the same as putting a clarinet reed on a clarinet mouthpiece; you'd put it just exactly even, not any higher or
lower.'

'Art who?' Jack said.

'Hazard,' Rick said.

'Not Art Hazard, not the real one?' Jack said,
holding the paper cup away from him and looking at
Rick with real interest. The rest of them were around
the jug too, and it was no longer a private conversation.
'What about Hazard?' one of them said.

'Sure,' Rick said, 'that's the one; there's only one
of them.'

'Well,' Jack said, 'I'll be damned.' He turned to the
whole group and said to them, 'This fella learned to
play trumpet from Art Hazard, what do you know?'
He turned to Rick. 'Why didn't you ever say anything about that before? How'd you happen to get to
know him in the first place?'

'Oh,' Rick said, embarrassed now because all of them
were looking at him, waiting for him to talk, 'he used
to live right near me, used to play at a little place in
Vernon.'

'The hell he did,' Jack said. 'I always supposed he
was from the East. What band?'

'Jeff Williams,' Rick said. 'It was the same bunch
that's playing with him now, but there were only five
of them then. They got a lot of new guys now but the
original five are all still with him. Ward, the first

drummer he had, died and he got Jordan, but Jordan played drums for him for two years before they went East, so one way you think of it, he's part of the original band too.'

Jack seemed mixed up. He was beginning to feel the gin. 'You mean to tell me a white man would play in a coon band? Art Hazard really plays for Jeff Williams?'

'Hazard isn't white,' Rick said.

'You mean Art Hazard isn't a white man?' Jack said, his jaw way down.

'Heck no,' Rick said, and Tracy, the drummer, backed him up. 'He's black as your hat. Haven't you ever seen a picture of him? He's a nigger, all right.'

'Well, anyhow, he doesn't play in Williams's band now,' Jack said. 'He gets out his own records: Art Hazard's Rhythm Band. I've got a couple of them myself and I'll show you.'

'That's just to get around a contract,' Rick said. 'Williams is under contract to get out two records a month, but he can make as many as he wants under a different name. He's made a lot under different names. Did you ever hear of Smoke Jordan's Dixie Blazers? That's Williams. Or Snowden's Cotton Pickers? That's Williams. It's all the same band. You can tell if you listen to it. Nobody else plays that way.'

'Maybe so,' Jack said. 'So Art Hazard's a nigger?'

He shook his head. 'Next thing you'll be telling me Red Nichols is a nigger.'

'Oh, no,' Rick said, 'Red Nichols isn't.'

All of them laughed and Jack looked happier. He hated like poison not to be a smart boy all the time. 'I'm glad I've got you here to tell me about Nichols,' Jack said to enforce his advantage. And when Rick saw that he was taking a boobing he simply said, 'Oh, I thought maybe you really didn't know,' and the thing was turned around again and Jack was glowering.

Everybody began to feel the strain, and nobody wanted to. The result was that each man hit the gin as a kind of insurance against strife in their midst; and the gin, in its turn, hit each man according to his temperament and special aptitudes. The rehearsal had its ups and downs. Rick went carefree, but only to a certain point. He stopped caring what Jack thought about Jeff's band, he didn't let Jack's musical standards bother him, he didn't let anything bother him. He acquiesced to the leader very simply and kept on playing the arrangements for what there was in them and for what he could get out of them. And because he couldn't get in any licks and couldn't improvise, he gave himself to tone. He got a quality into his playing and a tone out of his horn that melted Jack Stuart's heart, and at the end of another hour and three more gins there he was again in excellent repute, top man in the show from anybody's point of view. Jack did him honor. He broke down and said: 'Boy, they told me right about you. You could take a seat in any band in the country.'

At two o'clock there were three of them left, Rick and Eddie Phelps and Tommy Long, the guitar player. The rest of them had gone under one by one; some had just wandered off and hadn't come back; others had left in a hurry and hadn't come back either. Jack had taken Jones home. He said he'd come back but he didn't. And then there were three, all three good and drunk but still able to play. They folded up the music and did a home-made job. They'd start something, play three choruses of it, ease down as if to break it off, and then one of them would take it again, just for a final run, and at the end of that one somebody else would get another idea and pick it up again. Perpetual motion. When they finally got it stopped, they'd just sit there and laugh like mad until they started to play again.

But things like that can't go on forever. Comes a point where change is bound to occur. Tommy Long's little finger began to bleed where the guitar strings had cut it through. 'I gotta quit,' he said, 'or I'll be getting blood all over my new guitar.'

'I'd just as soon quit,' Rick said. 'I can take it or leave it alone.'

Phelps didn't say anything. His face was tomato red and his shirt was soaked from armpits to belt. Tommy gave him a slap on the stomach and it sounded like a wet towel. 'You get yourself all warmed up, don't you?' he said.

'I'll say,' Eddie said. 'I've been this way all my life. I had to quit dancing because I was always in an awful shape after just one dance.'

Rick was wiping off his trumpet and putting it away. 'They say,' he said, 'it's a sign you're healthy if you can sweat a lot. When you get so you can't sweat, you die.'

He was measuring out his words one after the other, as if the only way he could manage the breath to talk was to take it slowly, one step at a time. 'I hardly sweat at all, anytime. I get so hot I could blow my top but I just don't sweat,' he said.

Phelps was pulling his shirt away from his ribs. 'I sure do,' he said. 'It might be a good idea to go swimming now; cool off.'

It was about half-past three then, that unclassified and unadaptable time of night which traditionally is no proper time to retire, and yet no time to start the day. It looked like a good time to go swimming, and the three who survived the rehearsal walked to the bay. Placid water, they felt, would suit their purpose better than the smashing surf.

They undressed on the boathouse float. There was no moon and the water at the edge of the float was black. Phelps went off with a splash and made a sound of surprise. Then Tommy Long got in and said Jesus.

Rick stood naked and apprehensive and called out with fake heartiness, 'How is it?' And Phelps's voice came back carrying a phrase frightful in implication: 'It's wonderful once you get in. Come on.'

Rick sat down on the edge of the float and immersed his legs up to the knees. 'Oh, God,' he whispered with the beginning of a sob. Then he recalled with coward's pleasure that this water would be deep, twenty times as deep as he was, God knows, eighty maybe, and he with a bare knowledge of how to tread water. Get yourself drowned. Only fools rock the boat. Bad business. He pulled his legs up, found his own shoes and socks, and put them on and felt himself a man once more — a man with his shoes on.

He stood there single and whole, a little man on a wooden float that lay on the surface of a great ocean beneath a night that was as big as all outdoors. His arms were folded across his bare chest, his feet were farther apart than need was to brace him against the gentle rocking of the float, and he looked upward at the stars that were stuck into the night. But not humbly, not like Pascal. The eternal silence of those infinite spaces did not move him to fear. Lunks of stars — no brains, no ability, no senses — just nothing but simple chunks of matter kicking around in space. He was as steadfast as they were, and he could think and talk and know who he was besides. What, after all, has a star got?

Pretty, though. Stand there and look at them and they get prettier and prettier, almost pretty enough to persuade you. Rick kept his face turned upward and shifted his feet farther apart to brace himself against an inward rocking that was a personal matter and had nothing to do with the float. The breeze was soft, and it had just enough movement to bring him constantly a new touch and a reminder that it was there with him. Funny thing about stars on a black night, they put you in mind of other things, things like the stars only so much more complicated. Where, for instance, is there a girl who will have this same cool brilliance? What would her name be? How do you inquire for her?

After an endless time of standing, he went down, lay back and let the night fall over him, and he was cured, then, of inward rocking. He lay still on his back, looking up, aspiring, and without any fanfare about it he knew everything at once. He thought it out without words, the way music thinks — in depths and currents that have nothing to do with linguistics. In these gracious terms he knew that there was good in the world, and tenderness, and sadness; and when it can be said of you that you know anything at all, you will know what these things are.

The float lurched, and Eddie Phelps pulled himself up and spattered water all over when he stumbled against one of Rick's feet. There were questions, then, and answers, and all sorts of talk; and then Tommy

Long pulled himself aboard too, and there was dressing and huffing and puffing, but none of it mattered, and Rick Martin walked back to the house, troubled slightly, as if he'd missed something big by a very little.

2

IT TURNED out precisely the way the man at the soda fountain had said it would. Schools began to close down at the end of the first week in June and then Balboa was a hive, but not of industry. The beach was a solid half-mile of striped canvas umbrellas, and each umbrella functioned as base for a group of boys or girls or boys and girls held together by some tie or other, friendship, love, fraternity, chance, or plain sodality. The wonderful thing was that a man could leave his base and go down to the sea to swim and cool off, and find his way back, apparently, to the same umbrella and the same people he had left. You wouldn't believe, just to look at all those striped umbrellas and all those bare legs stretched out like spokes in the sand below them, that there could be differentiations, that it would matter much whether a man found his way back to one or to another.

At night it was much the same thing except that the center of things was not the beach but the Rendez-Vous ballroom. At night, instead of lying prone on their stomachs in the sand, the youths and maidens stood upright on their feet and danced to the music. Two-

bits per capita admission, and five cents a dance;
sailors, but no holds, barred. The Rendez-Vous had not
been let out an inch too much by that real-estate man
from Los Angeles; the Collegians played to a capacity
crowd on Saturday nights, Sunday afternoons, and
Sunday nights, and they got a good crowd on week
nights too after the first of the season. They got
Monday night off, and needed it.

It was a good-looking band; not a bald head in the
bunch, not a paunch in the lot. They wore white
flannels and blue and white blazers and black and white
shoes, and they looked, individually, right in them,
which is a hard thing, as a rule, for any ten men to do
at the same time. Their pictures, singly and group-shot,
were put up beside the entrance, retouched until you
could scarcely tell Jack from Rick or Phelps from Long.

Their music was what Jack wanted it to be, smooth
and expressive of collegiate emotion. Maybe it was
better than that; it was good enough, in any case, to
draw an occasional party from Hollywood. The rumor
went that Buster Keaton came down to dance almost
every week end, and with that for a lead rumor ran
rife. The Rendez-Vous became, less than three weeks
out, a famous place to dance. Some of the rumors may
even have had a basis in fact.

It was sometime around in here that Rick began to
turn out his famous solo work, and it got started in a
strange way. The boys in the band, most of them, had

established romantic liaisons with girls on the beach early in the season, and every night as the night's work wore on, all of them would get unbearable inclinations to jump ship and go dance. It bothered them to sit there and play music while other men danced with their girls. So they worked out a system. Every fourth number was a waltz; the saxophones would take one out, the brass the next, tuba drums and guitar fixed it up among them, and Rick, who didn't care about leaving the stand often, doubled on piano when Jack danced. It didn't disrupt the band badly; they played three fox trots in a row, tutti ensemble, and the waltzes didn't matter much. From a dancing point of view there's no crying need of a full orchestra for a waltz. They even stopped using scores for waltzes, and took to playing 'Sweetheart of Sigma Chi,' 'Roses of Picardy,' 'I Love You Truly,' and others of that stripe in medleys.

But one time when Jack was off and Rick was supposed to play piano while Tommy played the violin in front of a bank of reeds, Rick let the reeds go too, and told Tommy to put away that violin and play guitar while he played trumpet. He pulled the tuba and drums in close, the four of them in a half-circle, and he told them what to do and they did it. They gave out the rhythm and he played, not in three-four time, but very slow four-four, an old tune called 'Japanese Sandman.' He played it straight as the crow flies, and clear, to be heard distinctly all over the hall, but there was a push behind it and a lift to it and a measured clarity that made something happen in that long, narrow Rendez-Vous ballroom. He finished three choruses and lost his nerve, jumped at the piano, handed Tommy his violin and bow, and went as if to underbrush into the opening bars of 'I Love You Truly,' waltz time.

But the thunderbolt he expected never came. When Jack came back and gave him a curious look, Rick gulped and made introductory vowel sounds trying to think what to say for himself, and all Jack said was: 'Mary-Lou's back from San Francisco already, she just came in, and now I'm going to be in a hell of a mess with Barbara. I've got to think of something quick.'

Rick pulled his sleeve across his mouth and didn't have to say a thing. He just sat in his chair and made his plans. He felt like a kid that has just happened to look down and see a dollar lying in the gutter at the corner of Sixth and Main.

He sat through the next three numbers and thought it all out, and at the end of three when Jack said to him man to man, 'What would you do?' Rick said: 'Go dance with her and tell her you were lonesome and here was this other babe going for you and nothing you could do. Just tell her how it was.'

'Sure,' Jack said. 'Only I think Barbara's so much cuter than Mary-Lou now.'

'She's cuter all right,' Rick said. 'Why don't you go dance with *her* then and tell her you were stuck with Mary-Lou before you saw her and now you'll try to fix everything up? Go on, dance with her.'

Jack pulled himself together and said: 'Look here, I can't leave you stuck all the time, just because you're big-hearted. It's time you took one off. Maybe I'd be better off not to see either of them.'

And Rick, keeping his voice level and managing somehow to make it sound natural, said: 'Hell, Jack, I can't dance. I'd just as soon play for you every time, and if I didn't mean it I wouldn't say it. Go on, dance with Barbara and tell her how the whole thing happened before it's too late and she's sore. Go ahead, or you won't be able to find her.'

'All right, then,' Jack said. 'I guess you're right.' He got away fast and Rick turned around and let everybody go except Tommy and Staats Tracy, the drummer. Tracy had overtime coming to him, and there was a little argument, but Rick wouldn't back down. Tommy had some time coming, too, but he didn't say anything about his; he had a sense that something would come of this and he'd just as soon be in on it. Rick turned to Tracy and said, 'Beat out four bars alone; and then you,' he said to Tommy, 'come in with him for two more, slow fox-trot, and then I'll come in.' He had them listening to him as if he were giving out official, last-minute instructions for a *coup d'état.* 'How slow?' Tracy asked him, and Rick slapped his thigh twice, explicit answer. 'What key?' Tommy said, and when he saw in Rick's face that it was no matter, he changed it and said, 'What tune?' and Rick said, 'Oh, something.' He couldn't think what; all he could think was how.

So Tracy led them out and the first dancers came onto the floor, and Tommy came in and established a key, and Rick held his trumpet up sideways, to take a fast look at it, and then he began to play. There wasn't anything settled in his mind yet, as far as tune went, and so he just played notes in patterns, introducing himself until something clicked into the slot and he was playing one that Smoke had liked two years before called 'Swinging' (I believe) 'down the Lane.'

Rick was shot full of tact. He hadn't known what he was going to play, but when he played it finally, it was one that Jack would have to like, it was this good flowing little tune that didn't have a jot of meanness in it, and he could shade it off and lift it up and do right by the simplicity of it. The music flowed out over the dancers and a kind of peace held forth, for the moment, in the Rendez-Vous. Here was music that could be tender and still hold its shape, keep firm its contour, and that's a thing that 'I Love You Truly' played by three saxophones and a violin can't do. Four choruses of 'Swinging down the Lane' had the crowd. They didn't listen to it, especially, but when Rick stopped playing they wouldn't leave the floor, they wanted whatever it was to keep on. They just stood still in their places and clapped steadily. The floor boys unhooked the ropes and stood by to let the dancers leave the floor; and then they walked in toward the center of the floor in a gesture of forcing them to leave, but no. The dancers simply stood their ground and clapped their hands. It looked like a token.

It felt like so many claps on the back. Here was recommendation, commendation, applause. And Tommy Long, in official capacity as accompanist, leaned back and gave the soloist an actual clap on the back and said, 'Nice going, boy!'

The big thing, however, was that Jack Stuart edged himself up through the crowd dragging Mary-Lou or Barbara with him, and gave him a sign to take an encore. Rick played four more choruses, and in return for the encouragement he turned out some very, very nice work. At the end of four his nerve broke a little and he got up quickly, put his trumpet on his chair, and left by the back door. As soon as he closed the door, he lighted a cigarette, blew the smoke sky high, and knew the difference between being a success and being kicked out. It left him a little fluttery in the stomach, things like that are so close. You're thrown out for insubordination or else you aren't, and where the actual line of demarcation stands out clear, God himself only can know. The only way to find out approximately, even, is to try something funny and see if you get away with it. And because you did once is no guarantee in writing that you will again. But Rick didn't look long at the negative side. All he knew was that recognition, that sweet thing, had been given to him because he had been doing some good playing. It's a simple formula: do your best and somebody might like it.

Tracy and Tommy came out and found him standing on the steps with his back to the wall. 'What did you want to quit for?' Tracy said. 'They kept on clapping for a hell of a time.' Tommy gave him another slap on the back and said, 'Yeh, I almost decided to play them a guitar solo.'

Rick couldn't say a thing. Jack came up through the passageway with Phelps and the rest of them, and when he came to Rick he came to an imponderable and had the sense not to ponder. 'Do that again sometime,' was all he said. And then Rick threw down his cigarette and walked back to the stand with him. He didn't try any explaining; he allowed himself his basic assumption — that it's unrewarding to play waltzes on the piano if you really know how to play a good trumpet — and he said: 'It would have sounded better if there'd been a piano in it. Guitar's hardly strong enough for a place this size, no matter how loud it's played.'

Jack nodded his head. He was doing some reconsidering. 'I'll play with you next time,' he said. 'You and me and guitar and drums, don't you think?' That, apparently, for Barbara; and that, too, for Mary-Lou. Man's work to be done. 'That would make it just about right,' Rick said.

Done. Every fourth dance, or just about every fourth dance, turned out to be a trumpet solo by Rick Martin, flanked by some rhythm. Jack may have brought himself to believe that every fourth dance was a piano solo by Jack Stuart, assisted by trumpet and guitar, but it wasn't. The precedent was established, nevertheless, no matter who thought what, and once a good precedent like this one really takes root it can thrive and flourish like this one. The dancers came to expect to hear Rick's trumpet in the small combination, and when the season was no more than a month out, the boys and their girls threw their tickets into the box when Rick's turn came, and pushed each other around trying to get up close to the stand to hear him play.

It's a strange thing. It might never have happened, and it might have been just as well if it never had happened to happen, but there it was; Rick Martin, the summer he was twenty, had already clicked.

Jack Stuart knew that he was blessed above the run of band leaders. It isn't given to all organizers to have a stand-out in their organizations. It's what makes the money roll in. Jack saw it sharply enough on the night of the token, and when Rick's success held up for another two weeks his course was clear. He had a picture of himself and Tracy and Tommy and Rick put up along with the other pictures at the entrance, under the caption: Featuring Jack Stuart's Oregon Four. He couldn't quite bring himself to give Rick a by-line, but he did give him a chance to play.

They were big days. Rick was on the way and he knew it, but not in definite terms. All he knew was that he was good and that he wanted to be better. The honest truth was that he wanted to be the best. Martin Maximus. At night after the hall had closed, he did whatever anybody invited him to do. He sat in back rooms and talked and drank with Tommy Long and Phelps and anybody else, or he drove to Wilmington or San Pedro with or for women. But when he woke up at the house, the first thing he knew was who he was and what he did for a living. It was in the daytime that he didn't do what anybody invited him to do. He consciously, and with stealth, tried to get away in the daytime. There was one, and only one, simple way to do this thing, and that was to get up early, to get up and leave the house between ten and ten-thirty in the morning, when no one else would think of such a thing. He liked everybody and everybody liked him, but all the same he had to get away, he needed some time to get his thinking done.

Outside, unshaven and unfed, he walked the longest way around to a fish and chips place on the bay, drank two cups of coffee and part of a third, and ate something easy. Then he got a shave the next block up and he was free for the day or as much of it as he wanted. He usually walked, then, all the way to the end of the peninsula and out to the end of the jetty. He didn't walk fast, he just kept going until he got to the end of the jetty, and then he sat down and looked at the water and watched far out for ships. Whenever he saw one his heart quickened, and that's about all the thinking he did. He just needed to have things quiet for a while and know who he was and what he was going to do about it, and he could get a better sense of it while he was looking at something good and big, like the Pacific Ocean. He built up a taste for the Pacific Ocean that nothing but the Pacific Ocean could satisfy. He got to it every day before noon, and sat clandestinely beside it for a long enough time to do him some good before he went back to Balboa.

It was probably the same thing that makes some people take naps in the afternoon or setting-up exercises in the morning or patent medicine — a double sense that one must neutralize past indulgence and prepare oneself for future ordeal. Parents foster it in children: drink your milk so your legs will be long, and if your legs get long enough goodness knows what you won't be able to do — ride a bicycle, climb trees, anything at all; but first drink your milk. In order to deal properly with the world the weak need something outside themselves to build up their nerve. The Pacific Ocean did it for a while for Rick. He sat beside it and took it easy.

That summer, too, he found a solace that held good for him all the rest of his life. It came about by pure chance. One of his Mondays off he went up to Long Beach on the Pacific Electric to look around in music stores and see what Hermie Klein's orchestra sounded like, and in the afternoon while he was walking around killing time, he got on a roller coaster for no reason that he knew — he'd never been on one before and he'd never wanted to. He knew it was all wrong the minute the thing started, but he was in it and his choice of alternatives was restricted; there was nothing to do but sit there and take it. He went crazy on the first dip, it hit him so hard he couldn't stand it and he was in something like a swoon until the thing stopped. He got off and held himself together for a block or two, but he was really shot and looking around for a straw to clutch at. What he saw was a sign for a Turkish bath and he thought maybe he could lie down in one, so he turned off the street and went down the stairs. He abandoned himself to rubbing and steaming; he got his nerve back and along with it a deep faith in Turkish baths. He never lost it. What men find in the church, in a mother, in all the offices of consolation and protection, Rick took out in Turkish baths.

With the summer solstice Balboa gathered its full force and Stuart's Collegians knew they were in the right place. The small combination in particular had Fortune smiling all over it. Rick got Phelps worked into it to give him something solid to play against, and then he was set. He was set in a mold then, as far as the rest of his life went.

It wasn't until about the eighth week that the slick fellow in the white linen suit came to talk business with Rick by way of Jack. He came up to the stand between numbers at about a quarter of one on a Saturday night and told Jack who he was. He was Lee Valentine, and he'd just finished two weeks of three-a-day at Grauman's Million-Dollar Theater. He'd been making stands at moving-picture houses all over the country for three months and he'd be going back to New York, thank God, in a week or two now. At the moment he was taking a rest and getting a chance to go around and hear how some of the other bands were doing. 'Nice band you've got,' he said.

Jack was the happiest of band leaders. Lee Valentine was a force among musicians. 'Thanks,' Jack said. 'I'm glad you like it.'

'I was wondering,' Valentine said, 'if you'd be interested in getting together after you're through; I thought we could have a drink or two some place and talk things over for a while.'

'I'll tell you,' Jack said. 'I have a kind of a date, but I think I could get out of it without much trouble. I'll sure try.'

'Oh, if you've got a date, why of course,' Mr. Valentine began; but Jack cut it off right there, and let it be known that he'd like much better to spend the evening with a fellow band leader, and of all fellow band leaders this very fellow band leader. 'Come back here in fifteen minutes,' he said. 'We quit at one; wait for me until I get it fixed.'

The man in the white suit walked off the floor, and Jack leaned over and said to Tommy Long, 'That guy was Lee Valentine,' and Tommy got it to Phelps, and Phelps to Jones, and Jones to Rick, and it went from him to the reed section and back by way of the drums. Jack called one, six, and ten for the last group instead of four, eight, and six as planned. Might as well play the best they had; put your most pleasing foot forward. The thought never came that they'd ever been listened to before right now, that it didn't make much difference which foot.

They played. Jack watched the floor like a hawk, but Valentine apparently wasn't dancing. When the last number was over, Rick and Jones went into their fanfare and the saxophones gave the answer: That's all; a high note and a low note. Jack left immediately to break his date. The rest of them pushed chairs around and removed mouthpieces and snapped cases and talked about what to do now. You could do one of two things, or both. Or if neither one had any appeal, you could go home and get some sleep because the next day would

be Sunday, and on Sunday it was a question of playing
straight through from two in the afternoon until one
at night. Sunday was the real day. 'Let's go around
to Aleck's and have a nightcap and go home, huh?'
Tommy said to Rick. 'Sure,' Rick said. He always did
what somebody else thought up. And at that moment
there was that man again, the one in the white linen
suit. He'd come to the stand by way of the back door
and he was standing by Rick and saying: 'Are you
Rick Martin? I know a fellow that knows you.'

'That right?' Rick said. 'Who?'

'Jeff Williams,' Valentine said. 'He told me you
were out here some place in a band, only he told me a
place in Ocean Park.'

'Sure, I know Jeff Williams,' Rick said. 'I used to
know him pretty well. He lived right near me.'

'That's what he said,' Valentine said. 'I found the
place in Ocean Park, all right, but you'd left it. Jeff
told me to look you up if I got a chance.'

Jeff Williams, it was easy to see, was in the eyes of
Lee Valentine a musician, not a negro. Valentine could
be free of the fraternity boy standards of Jack Stuart.
Jack Stuart himself might be free of them by the time
he'd been around as much as Lee Valentine.

'Do you know Jordan, plays drums for Jeff?' Rick
said.

'Smoke?' Valentine said. 'Sure I know him.'

'How is he?' Rick said.

'He's all right,' Valentine said. 'Fact is, he's the best drummer in the country.'

'I mean how's he getting along?'

Lee Valentine didn't make much of this either. 'They're all getting along all right,' he said. 'They're packing them in at the Old South, and have been all winter.'

'Well,' Rick said, and gave it up. He could write to Smoke if he wanted to know how he was.

'How many bands have you played in?' Valentine asked.

'Me?' Rick said. 'Oh, I've played jobs about twenty places. I've only worked steady at the Hawaiian Gardens and here with Stuart.'

'How in the world did you ever get mixed up with that Hawaiian Gardens outfit?' Valentine wanted to know. 'That's the saddest bunch I ever heard. The night I was down there the trombone was out in his chair; every once in a while he'd try to play for a minute or two, but he didn't have an idea where he was.'

'Gus,' Rick said. 'I know it. Nice guy, too, when you know him. He used to play with Tod Newsome when he was younger; they grew up together in the same town and stayed together for years, but I guess Gus got to be such a souse even Newsome had to kick him out. He's had a kind of a funny life.'

Jack Stuart came up behind them and said to Valentine, 'Let's go; I got it fixed.'

'Come on with us,' Valentine said to Rick; 'have a drink.' But Rick said he was going with Tommy and get home early on account of tomorrow being Sunday, thanks just the same.

Next morning Rick was up and fed and out on the jetty by ten o'clock. He watched the regatta — seven star-boats with immaculate white sails against a turquoise sea, and fourteen sportsmen taking chances on their only lives to find out which of them could get to Catalina first. He watched them until he couldn't extend his sight any further, and then he spent a lot of time thinking that it would be nice to have a telescope, one that he could let out until he got a squint at the place where those parallel lines meet when they're drawn out forever, ad infinitum, world without end. His eyes burned, feeling what that would look like; and then he had in its place a more real sense of time and space, the showman's instinct for the passing of time and precise estimate of how long it takes to get to looking like something in order to appear on time before the public eye. He stood up, tightened his belt, brushed off the seat of his pants, and started back to town.

When he went into the house, Jack Stuart, bleary in a white terry robe, came from his bedroom into the living-room and collapsed on the closest chair.

Rick was cheery and clear-eyed. 'How are you, kid?' he had the poor judgment to say to Jack.

'I'll say,' said Jack. And then he said what he remembered from the night before: 'Lee Valentine wants
to take you over, if you want to go.'

'Over where?'

'He wants to hire you, put you to work in his band.'

'Who said?'

'He said.' Jack held his head in his hands.

'No fooling?' Rick said.

'Yes,' Jack said systematically. 'No fooling. His
first trumpet ran out on him a week ago, got married
to somebody in the movies, nobody I ever heard tell of.
He tried out three trumpets last week and he didn't
want any of them, but he thinks you'd be all right. He
was at the hall all evening last night listening to us play.'

'He was?' Rick said. 'For God's sake.'

'So we talked it over last night, and I told him as far
as I was concerned I wouldn't stand in your way if you
wanted to go with him when he goes back to New York.
He's in a bad way with no trumpet.'

'What about our band here, though?' Rick said.
'We've got four more weeks; I can't quit.'

'Oh, I'll get along,' Jack said. 'I don't want to hold
you up.'

'Well,' Rick said, 'I like it here. We've got the
quartet all fixed up. We're doing fine. I couldn't quit
now, but thanks for telling me.'

Jack had a very bad headache and he wasn't in any
condition to go on being politic much longer.

'Sure, you'll quit,' he said. 'You've got to. Lee's stuck, and he says you'll do. I can get somebody to finish out this four weeks. He's a great guy and a good friend and I want to help him out of this. So you've got to go with him. If I'm willing I can't see why you aren't.'

He pulled himself up and went back into his bedroom and shut the door behind him. It had been a cash deal the night before; Jack had released his part of Rick for four hundred and seventy-five dollars in currency. The roll was in his pocket. Rick was sold whether he knew it or not. He had become, overnight, the property of Lee Valentine.

Book Four

Book Four

~~~~~~

1

IN BALBOA, California, in the month of August, the sea is blue and the breeze blows fresh, as opposed to the city of New York, where you wonder in the month of August how those long buildings can maintain their dignity.

Lee Valentine's band arrived in New York the eighth of August; and at five o'clock of the same day Rick Martin went, instructed, to be measured for a tuxedo and a tail coat. There were six days to kill before the band opened at the Porter Grille, free time except for rehearsals. It was a nice prospect, and when Rick came out on the street from the tailor's, he came out convinced that New York was, and would keep on being, his favorite place to live. He got it settled as quickly as that. It was too hot, but he didn't know it; in six months it would be too cold, and he wouldn't know that either. What had him was something in the air, nothing you could point to or say much about, just a sense of the imminence of everything anybody would want. Desiderata for the asking.

He didn't go back to the hotel, and he didn't go to the speakeasy where some of Valentine's boys were going to foregather at six. He had dinner and put in time until ten o'clock and then he went to the Old South Club. He looked up the address in a directory, and then he walked sixty blocks to get to it. It didn't occur to him to take a car; he started walking and saw that he was going in the right direction — at the end of each block the number went up one — and then he simply let himself glide the rest of the way in a daze, seeing nothing, hearing nothing, just getting himself to the Old South.

And when he got there he was afraid to go in, so he made it four more blocks walking around thinking it over. He didn't know what to expect inside. He didn't know whether it was a big nickel dance like the Rendez-Vous or whether it was one of those cabaret places where you have to call up first or whether it was just for negroes or white men could come in too. Maybe it was all white; no way of knowing. It was the right place, though, so much was sure. There was a small marquee extending out over some steps that led down half a flight to a shining black door with a silver cubistic design on it, and there was a doorman, a bright-looking negro boy in a red bell-hop's uniform. Rick straightened his tie and went down the stairs. The

negro boy didn't say stay out; he said good evening,
and held the door open.

It was dim inside, with blue lights cutting through
the smoke. Rick's pulse fluttered like a bird. When a
man came up to him and said, 'One?' Rick said one,
and then in a moment he was sitting at a small table,
about the fifth tier away from the floor. Through it all
the music was playing, and somewhere inside it there
was the meanest, rattiest, godawful lovely horn Rick
had heard since he'd heard the same one four years
before. And behind it all there was the kind of drum
beat that could send any band out of this world never
to return.

Rick looked at Smoke Jordan's black face shining
above that magnificent collection of white-skinned
drums, and he saw how much the same he was. Same
one that used to do the hot sweeping at Gandy's, only
that one wore yellow cords and this one wore a white
tuxedo. Daniel Jordan in a white tuxedo pounding
the prettiest set of drums in existence. A dazzling
sight. His eyes were turned obliquely upward and he
chewed his lower lip all the while he played; then he'd
knock out a beauty and turn his eyes down, startled,
as if he'd surprised even himself with that one. If
he knew Rick Martin was in the room would he play
any better or worse? He couldn't play any better.

Rick looked up and saw a waiter standing beside him
with the air of a waiter who has been waiting fifteen

minutes and is about to call the customer's attention by poking him one. 'Two gin fizzes,' Rick said. The waiter turned up the other chair and said, 'You're expecting someone?' 'No,' Rick said. 'Two for me.'

There were eight new men in the band, two trumpets and a trombone, four saxophones, and a string bass. But the original five were all there, as original as they'd ever been. They had a new system of taking solos standing up, and the solo takers were always the Los Angeles boys. Art Hazard was up now taking one for an awful ride. He was better than he used to be, probably; more assured, and along with it a little more spectacular. He was no longer a kid doing the best he could in a five-piece band in Vernon; he was a mature musician, a master who looked well on the way to becoming a past master. Of the five of them, he was the one who had changed the most. He was at least fifty pounds heavier than he'd been in Los Angeles, and he had a wise look on his face, as if he'd found out something or other about a way of living. He looked like a black Bacchus, a vile and merry man.

His was the last chorus, and when the music stopped the crowd went into a collective tantrum. They clapped, they whistled, they stomped; and when, as a pacifier, Arthur Hazard stood up again and repeated the last solo, there was no end to it. Rick didn't clap; he felt a wave of heat rise to his head, and he drank his second gin at one shot, like a glass of water, with the idea that the heat would go down with it. He was at home now, natural and right, and this was homecoming. The only home he'd ever known was this kind of music, and here it was, changeless and abiding. A solid structure with a light in the window.

Arthur Hazard was standing up there, his silver trumpet looking fragile between his hands, bowing to the right of him, bowing to the left of him, and loving it. He was the man of the evening, and this white crowd couldn't get enough of him.

There was a floor show at two, and at three the place closed. People went weaving out to get their hats, and Rick stood up, crossed the floor, jumped up to the stand, and said, 'How are you, kid?' to Smoke.

Smoke looked up, opened wide his eyes, and said, 'Well, I'll be good God damned,' in slow, measured syllables. 'Is that you?'

'Sure.'

They couldn't seem to think of anything else to say, but they didn't have to because in a moment everybody was there, ganged around Rick, shaking his hand and asking him what it was all about, how come he came to be in New York, when'd he get in?

Rick told it, and when he'd finished, Jeff said: 'Valentine, huh? What you doing for him?'

'First trumpet,' Rick said.

'Boy, you must have got good getting a job like that,' Jeff said.

Valentine said you told him to look me up's why he ever happened to.'

And Jeff said that Art had had a part in it too. They all got to figuring he was probably getting good by this time, and they told Lee when he left.

They stayed at the Old South for another hour, just talking things over, and from there they went to another place in Harlem, a black and white place called the Domino, and at one time they were in a place called Galba's, and there was some music there. It was a celebration, a gala night of it, old acquaintance not forgot, and at seven-thirty Smoke and Rick were walking up Lennox Avenue, tacking once in a while, but most of the time going straight ahead. The rest of the band had dispersed somehow, and there were left just these two, Smoke still wearing his white tuxedo.

'Let's go get us some chow mein,' Smoke said.

'We just had some,' Rick said.

'What a memory!'

It was a bright summer morning, already hot, and they were walking it off and getting steadier and more rational all the time. But it didn't matter; for them, in those days, reality was just as good as hallucination. The world looked all right any way they chose to look at it. They could stand it as it was, or completely out of focus and heavily veiled.

'Let's go get us some peanuts, then,' Smoke said. 'We ain't had any of them yet, have we?'

But there wasn't any peanut place and Smoke went on talking and talking, saying boy, did you wow them! Did you wowm there at Galba's.

'Wow who?'

Rick couldn't seem to remember anything about it, but that was one part of the night that Smoke knew everything about. They'd got into Louie Galba's place, a little sixth-floor salon with a platform no bigger than six feet square with a studio piano on it and a set of traps and Louie Galba sitting on a kitchen chair balanced right on the edge of the platform playing a trumpet while some woman sang a slow song. When the song was finished, Louie came over and set them all up a drink, and then everybody set everybody else up two or three more and Jeff told Louie that Rick was in New York to play trumpet. 'Go on, then,' Louie said, 'play mine for a while.'

'Can't remember a thing about it,' Rick said. But as he said it he caught the memory in the muscles around his mouth and he knew it was true. Smoke said there was no doubt about it, that he tore the place wide open; that horn of Galba's never trafficked in anything like it before, and everybody there knew it. Everybody was asking Jeff who he was, where he came from, and Hazard told them all that he himself raised that boy up, taught him to play a horn when he was so little he couldn't hold it up, he had to rig him up a couple of apple boxes to carry the weight of it. Yes sir. He taught him how. He showed him the way.

'I guess that's damned near true,' Rick said. And
Smoke said come off it, nobody could ever teach him
nothing. What he played last night he couldn't have
learned off of no guy, not even Hazard. It's something
a man's got to put in by himself, when it's like that.
You don't learn it, you make it.

'I guess I must have been sort of tight,' Rick said.

'Funny you didn't seem tight,' Smoke said. 'Too
bad you can't remember, because you sure did wowm.'

'I like this town,' Rick said. 'Too bad we can't find
you a peanut wagon, though. Place this size.'

Smoke said he wasn't no woman, he could get his
mind off a thing if it wasn't handy, and right out of
that he said that he bet by four o'clock this afternoon
there wouldn't be a good musician in town that hadn't
heard about Rick at Galba's last night. There were a
lot of them there. There were always a lot of musicians
at Galba's; they didn't come to hear Louie; he was all
right, but who they came to hear was that girl sing.
Lou Marble, that long, narrow girl that was singing
when they came in, the one that gave them the dirty
look when Jimmy Snowden tipped over his chair leaning back. She was what they came to hear; she was
sort of a secret. Louie wanted everybody to hear her,
but he kept his fingers crossed hoping nobody'd hear
her who could offer her a lot more money. That's what
happened to the last girl he had singing at his place;
some show fellow saw her and gave her a part in a play,

not even singing, and she's a big-time actress now, what the hell's her name? Then Louie found this one; he had a way of finding girls, but she had him really scared; she's too good. He knew somebody'd come along and take her away, just any time now.

Rick thought hard and said he guessed maybe he did remember her a little. He could call back a slow, tired voice, soft and damp like a fog. He could call it almost all the way back when he really tried.

But when Rick started playing Louie Galba's trumpet, Lou Marble's star was blacked out for the evening. She didn't even care, when he really got going, whether it was or not. She was the first one that came over to Jeff and asked who Rick was, where he came from, how he happened to be in town and nobody'd ever heard him.

'No fooling?' Rick said.

'God's my judge,' Smoke said.

They were stopped at a corner, each of them leaning an elbow against one side of a mail-box. They stood there a long time before Rick said: 'Whyn't we get going? What're we waiting for?'

'Here's where I live,' Smoke said, jerking his head toward the four-story flat-front house on the corner. 'I got an apartment in here. You want to come up?'

Rick said yes, very simply and honestly, and followed Smoke up three flights of circular stairs. Smoke found a key, unlocked the door, and pushed it open for Rick to enter.

It was a large, high-ceilinged room with two tall windows facing the Avenue. Opposite the windows there was a glazed-tile fireplace with a gas stove set into the opening. The walls were covered with plain yellow paper, very pleasant. Rick went straight to the mantel to look closer at a photograph in an elaborate stand frame. It was Josephine, full length, wearing what must have been a peacock costume — cut-away skirt of plumes erect behind her, fan shaped; bejewelled brassière, crested head-piece, and spike-heeled pumps. Nice outfit. Slanting across the bottom there was an inscription in loose, undisciplined handwriting: 'To my brother Dan, love Josephine.' A modest sentiment from one whose face was pure, direct, old-line heathen.

'Where'd she get the get-up?' Rick said, and Smoke answered from another room that she'd worn it in a revue at the Club Alabam when she was in the chorus there, and she had the picture made to send to the folks for Christmas to show them she was getting along all right. And two days after she sent it the Alabam closed and she didn't get a lick of work for damn near three months. Then she got a job checking hats at the Royale and then she sold cigarettes there, and finally she got a job singing from four to six at an uptown speakeasy. She had the kind of guts it takes to get along; no need to worry about her.

Smoke came into the room wearing a pair of gray

trousers and a white jersey. He was talking into a towel, and when he took it away from his face he saw Rick stretched flat on the couch, asleep. One hand was clenched on his chest and the other hung limp over the edge of the couch. Smoke looked down at his clear, serious face and heard the regular up-beat of his breathing. Then he went back to the bedroom and got some sleep himself.

2

IT DIDN'T take long. Fortune, in its workings, has something in common with a slot-machine. There are those who can bait it forever and never get more than an odd assortment of lemons for their pains; but once in a while there will come a man for whom all the grooves will line up, and when that happens there's no end to the showering down.

Somehow Rick became known. It started the first night at Louie Galba's, and there was no stopping it after that. It went along something like that stock sequence they use in the movies to show that news is being spread: copy men at their desks, then papers tumbling off the press, newsboys shouting their heads off, customers hunting for their nickels, and standing out above everything: the headline.

He was a musician's musician, that's how it started. The boys in the trade accepted him the way they'd accept a flawless reed or an improved mouthpiece.

Nobody resented him, because he'd sprung full-blown into New York. Nobody, except Jeff and Smoke and Hazard, had known him when; he hadn't climbed up over anybody's head. He just appeared and took his rightful place and stayed in it. There was a lot of excitement about it at first; there was the shock of discovering him, hearing him for the first time, telling somebody else to go hear him. And then in a year, or make it two, everybody had heard him and he had become a mark to shoot at, a standard to measure by. When he was twenty-four he was head man in the trumpet-playing business in this country, which is to say in the world. He never got much better than he was at Galba's that first night, he never got very much better than he was at the Rendez-Vous in Balboa. The main difference was that by the time he was twenty-four he was known, his name was known, and when he played you listened. He had a hundred thousand friends and the weather was always fair. You'd hear musicians say of a young comer, 'He's all right, but he's nobody's Rick Martin,' in the same way you hear another kind of connoisseur say, 'She has a certain talent, but she's no Duse.' The big name.

He hadn't changed much. He looked almost the same except that he was thinner. All the boyish imprecision of line was gone and he had hardened into what he was. He was sharp and firm and thin, and his eyes were as hard and bright as copper in the sun.

He was playing in Phil Morrison's orchestra when he was twenty-four, and he was making more money than he had time to spend. He could just about name his price at that point, but he never did. Phil kept things nice for him, and he worked hard for Phil.

There were twenty men in Morrison's orchestra, and two arrangers, one girl vocalist and a vocal trio. It was an organization, and almost as businesslike as an insurance company. They rehearsed three afternoons a week and Morrison drove them like slaves. But when they were on the stand everything worked like a charm; the boys knew what was wanted, and Phil Morrison stood up in front aimlessly waving a stick, so genial and relaxed that you'd get the idea he didn't know what was going on. Not so, though; one false move in that band and you were seeking employment.

Phil played his own arrangers' arrangements of popular tunes hot off the press. Any song he bought automatically had a good run; and he took them as they came, popular favorites all, played them for a month, and then shuffled them, one by one, off the bottom of the deck to make room for next month's batch. He had them pretty heavily arranged, with a transitional passage before every vocal, a new key for every chorus, and a grandiose finale, usually with some bells in it somewhere. This was his stock in trade, the standard product, and he was known for it. His orchestra held the established first place among society orchestras for years and years. And for a big orchestra, and a society orchestra, it was good. The way Rick Martin's trumpet used to spring up above the rest of their heads would make you think it was a great orchestra, and Rick wasn't the only good man in it, either; there was a fiddler who made you think twice, and a man who blew as good a trombone as you'll hear anywhere in public. But it wouldn't do to call it a great orchestra because it pandered to all tastes and there was always that grandiose ending. It was just a good big orchestra, playing out its nightly schedule at one big hotel or another, working for money, drawing a crowd, getting people out on the floor. But when that thin blond boy stood up in his place and tore off sixteen bars in his own free style, filling in the blank that was allotted to him on the score, it was a surprise forever, like seeing an airplane take off from the deck of a good solid ship. To hell, please, with the law of gravity.

The orchestra played from seven until one, but from seven until nine it was just Phil and enough of the boys to play for the dinner crowd. Rick never went to work until nine, when the serious dining was over and night life was about to begin. Then he played for four hours, almost without a break, because he worked in all the intermissions laying down backgrounds for the trio, doing odd jobs, playing straight solos. At one they quit for the night, and he was always just hitting his stride, so he went somewhere else. He lived his life after hours. After his good work was done he did better work.

It was at Louie Galba's one night at about two-thirty that he met Amy North. She and Josephine Jordan came in together. Rick and Louie Galba and Jimmy Snowden and Milt Barrow, who played clarinet in Johnny Deane's band, were all sitting on the edge of the little platform jamming away four at a time on an old tune that didn't mind being slapped around, didn't mind being unrecognizable. Jeff was playing piano for them and Smoke was playing drums. And right in the middle of it, the door opened and in came these two, apparently sober and in their right minds. Josephine, wearing a long blue dress and a squirrel coat, automatically flashed a smile around the room and then went to a little table back in a corner. The white girl followed her. She was wearing a rain coat and a black felt riding hat turned down all the way around. She took the hat off while she was crossing the room and brushed the rain from it. Her hair was light, nearly red, and she wore it parted on one side and brushed back sleek and straight behind her ears and knotted at the back of her neck. She looked like an English girl about to go out for a day's shooting, but she was American, and I don't think it was very clear to her then what she was out to do.

A waiter came up to their table. The girl talked it

over with Josephine and gave the order, and when they
had their drinks they touched glasses lightly and drank
to something or other in all seriousness. To crime,
possibly; or to success, or to interracial understanding.
Mud in your eye, in one form or another — I give you
Josephine Jordan and Amy North, the heathen and
the English-looking.

There were about thirty people left at Galba's, and six
of them were making music for the other twenty-four
to listen to, just playing for fun. Galba's was almost
wholly a musicians' hang-out by that time of night.
There were always a lot of women around, but even
so, the place had a kind of inner-sanctum air. When
the music stopped and Rick put his horn under his
arm and went back to his table to get a drink, the rest
of them followed; then somebody over on the far side
of the room yelled Jo, and then somebody else yelled
Jo, and in a minute the room was full of it.

'I guess that's my ticket,' Josephine said. 'I guess
I've got to go sing. We should have known better
than to come here.' But she didn't hang back. She
slipped the squirrel coat from her shoulders and stood
forth in her long blue dress, and there was a great shout
for her. She motioned to Jeff as she crossed the
room.

Amy North drank off her drink, called the waiter,
and moved to the other side of the table, facing the
music. There are various ways of showing off, and one

of them is not to show off. You couldn't tell about Amy
North; she sat there, both hands on the table, not
moving a muscle, only watching Josephine as if she
were a horse she'd just put her last cent on.

There was a conference in front of the platform,
Josephine talking it over with Jeff and Louie Galba;
then something was decided and Jeff jumped up on the
platform and held his hand out to Josephine while she
climbed the two steps, and Louie Galba silenced the
people, saying, 'Ladies and Gentlemen ...' (Applause.)
'We are about to hear the song "I'm in Big Trouble,"
sung by the star of the show Big Trouble, Miss ...
Josephine ... Jordan.' (Applause.)

Jeff, sitting very straight at the piano, played out a
slow introduction; Josephine, standing at the edge of
the platform, swayed slightly, closed her eyes halfway,
and began her song:

> This room is cold
> And I'm in trouble.

She sang it quietly, and you could hear every word
as if she were close to you, talking to you. She stood,
swaying in her long blue dress, sleek and tall, her bare
brown arms slightly raised from her sides in a way they'd
taught her. But they hadn't taught her to do what she
was doing with the song, they hadn't taught her to
sing The room is cold, the streets are wet, I'm here
alone, babe, did you forget? and make it stand for

all the trust and all the betrayals of all time. It was the true, tragic thing, from her mouth, and to hear it was to know it.

She bowed when it was over, ducking slightly at the knees three times, left, center, right, and then she turned around and thanked Jeff and started to go down the steps. But they didn't want her to, the customers made an awful commotion. Josephine went back and made bows again, and smiled directly at Amy North. Then she turned around and conferred with Jeff, and in a moment he motioned to Rick, who was sitting with Milt Barrow and Smoke. There was another conference, very short, and Louie Galba told the customers that Jeff Williams and Josephine Jordan and Rick Martin were going to try to remember how they did their last record and do it that way again. 'Four or Five Times' was the title, an Orpheum Record released this week; Josephine Jordan and Her Play Boys; and incidentally it won't make Miss Jordan sore if you rush right out and buy this one. (Laughter.)

They played that and three more, and then Josephine said she'd had enough, whether anybody else had or not; what she needed was a drink with a lot of gin in it. 'Get Danny and come over to my table,' she said halfway between Jeff and Rick. Jeff went back with her and Rick went to get Smoke.

When Rick and Smoke came back, the table was being reorganized, going into a merger with another

one to make room. The white girl between Jeff and
Josephine had taken off her coat.

'This is my brother, Dan Jordan,' Josephine said to
Amy. 'And this is Professor Martin, Doctor North.'
Amy smiled at Smoke, and then turned to Rick and
said, 'I'm charmed, Professor,' and Rick said something
or other, nothing much, in return. He was looking
back at the platform, watching Milt Barrow and Louie
and a couple of men from Freeman's getting ready to
play. 'Who's the guy with the sax?' he said to Smoke,
and Smoke said some friend of Abe's, just in from
Chicago and supposed to be good.

Everybody sat down then and ordered. Rick seemed
to feel that the evening was over; he yawned, stretched
his legs under the table until they got tangled with
Amy North's feet; then he sat up straight again,
lighted a cigarette, and had the package back in his
pocket when he saw that Amy North had the look of
wanting a cigarette. So he fetched out the package
again and held it out to her.

Jeff and Amy were on one side of the table, Rick and
Josephine across from them, and Smoke at the end
next to Rick.

'Remember Ferry, used to play piano for Valentine?'
Rick said to Smoke. 'He's dead.' And when Smoke
asked how and when, Rick said: 'Last week sometime.
He quit Lee and bought a car and he was driving out
to California with the top down and a train hit him.

Somewhere in Kansas. Only way they're sure it was
him, they found his union card.'

'I'll be damned,' Smoke said, and Josephine said,
'Was he the good-looking one that played with Valentine, or the other one?'

'The other one,' Rick said. 'Ferry was a funny-
looking guy, and crazy as hell, too. He used to walk
everywhere, couldn't stand to be in the back of a taxi;
if he had to take one he'd always sit up front with the
driver, it drove him nuts in back; and he used to walk
up to the eighth floor of the hotel all the time, because
he didn't like elevators. The bars, or something. Once
we took him home drunk and put him in the elevator
and he opened his eyes just as the door closed and he
made a terrible squawk. We had to hold him until we
got to his floor. And he'd always get somebody else
to go in a phone booth and phone for him. God, I've
made some silly calls for that guy in my time.'

'Did he like to be in any room at all?' Amy North
asked. Her voice was mid-register, and she used just
enough of it to make herself heard.

'No, he didn't,' Rick said, 'much. He used to sit
in the park quite a lot.'

'Claustrophobia,' the girl pronounced it.

'What did you say?' Rick said, and all of them looked
at her.

'It's rather a common thing,' said Amy North looking
down into her glass. 'I don't like telephone booths

much, myself. I always get the feeling when I'm in one that it might fall down, and there I'd be, flat on my back in a telephone booth. They're too narrow; you can't raise your arms straight out.'

'Oh, well,' Josephine said, 'you can always phone in them, and that's all they're supposed to be for.' She looked around the table and said: 'This is the way she gets when she remembers she's a doctor. Sometimes she's nice.'

The two of them exchanged a look, and Amy said, 'It's big of you to say so.'

'Are you a doctor?' Rick said.

'No,' Amy said. 'I'm not.'

'Well, she's going to be,' Josephine said. 'Aren't you? Or what was it?'

'I wrote it down for you only yesterday.'

'Well, anyhow, she's going to hypnotize people and get them to say what balled them up when they were kids. Isn't that it?'

They looked at each other and laughed as if Josephine had said something pretty funny; Rick and Smoke and Jeff sat there looking troubled.

'Maybe we need a drink,' Rick said. He called the waiter.

'Once I saw a man hypnotize a woman in the window of Rogers' Dollar Store,' Smoke said. 'They left her in there two days and nights, asleep on a couch in there, and she stayed asleep the whole time, because

my brother Nathan set the alarm for two o'clock one
night and went down to see if it was a fake or not, and
she was in there asleep, all right. Then the next afternoon the guy that did it stepped into the window and
snapped his fingers in front of her teeth and she sat
right up and smiled.'

'There used to be an act that went on just before us,
when we were on tour,' Rick said. 'This fellow got
people to come up out of the audience and then he'd
make them do all kinds of things. I got to know him
on the train; he'd been to school in Austria and studied
psychology, but something went wrong and he ended
up with this act. He took morphine; he was sick once
and he had me get some for him. He didn't want anybody to find it out; but he just took a chance on me.'

'And so you sit here and tell everybody,' Amy
North said. 'Nice fellow.'

'It's all right now,' Rick said. 'He's been dead for
a year and a half.'

'That's a strange thing, too,' Amy North said. 'To
worm confidences out of people and wait around until
they die, and *then* tell.' She was looking into her glass
all the time, and whenever she spoke she got an oracular
quality into her voice. 'Very strange,' she said.

She was good-looking, like the line drawings of
girls in advertisements for too-expensive sweaters. She
was wearing one of those very sweaters, in fact, a gray-
blue one that looked as if it would feel like suds under

the hand. It made her look as if she'd got into the wrong room. She was twenty-four and pretty well used to being in the wrong.

She looked across at Josephine and said: 'Now Josephine's not that way; if she knew *I* took morphine — if she knew *anything* about me — she wouldn't tell it either now or after I'm dead. I'm sure of that.'

She looked away. Everybody sat still. Then Rick said: 'Hell, lady, I don't know what I said wrong. Everybody knew this fellow took morphine anyhow; he just liked to think nobody did. See one of his legs you'd know.'

Smoke broke in to say, 'He didn't say what the guy's name was, even; we were only talking about hypnotizing.'

Amy looked at Rick and said, 'You're slightly on the literal-minded side, aren't you, Professor? Don't take me seriously. I was just making talk.' She smiled at him, a pleasant smile, direct and candid. Her teeth were white and her mouth was clean. She stretched a hand toward him across the table.

Rick took it and said: 'I'm sorry. I really thought you meant it. I thought I gave you the idea that I went around making up lies about people and spreading them around.'

'Oh,' Amy said, 'then this man really didn't take morphine; you just made that up?'

'No,' Rick began, and then he pressed his lips together as if he couldn't make up his mind whether to hit her or not. 'Where's this getting us?' he said.

The girl looked at him closely again and said, 'I hadn't thought of that.' She gazed deep into her glass, thinking of it.

'When you get through having your fight,' Josephine said, 'I wish somebody around here would be man enough to order a drink.'

Jeff Williams was man enough to order one around and then go home. And then Smoke dropped out and Amy and Josephine and Rick were in a taxi, and then it was just Amy and Rick in a taxi and the rain was smashing in tubfuls against the glass trying to get at them.

But they were unassailable. The earth was turning well off center, so that time was forever and not made of minutes. The real world (the street lights, the flask, Rick's trumpet case) was as vague as the sound of tires whirling through water beneath them, but even then it seemed that the mind could slice like a knife through all the knots of syntax to make anything probable and everything communicable. And while this extraordinary lucidity held up, Amy North had things to communicate.

She sat holding Rick's silver flask in one hand and her hat in the other. When a light flashed up, Rick could see her head, disengaged from the rest of her and set in the bowl of her upturned coat collar. A strange girl with things on her mind. She was telling him now that thought is what matters, or thinking; the mind, in any event, is what matters. The world is in men's minds, and whoever can find the spring and discover the process, the method, the workings, will know everything. Who finds this out will have the world in a jug, Richard, do you know that? Who picks this out of the crannies will know what God and man is.

She stopped to think that one over, and Rick said quietly, 'Go on,' and she went on, spinning the three-thread twist of her thoughts and fallacies and counter-rationalizations out and out, her clear voice making smooth alcoholic periods.

She felt up to saying that she herself might be the one to find it if she worked as hard and with as much imagination as she intended to work. She'd go through with an M.D. simply in order to be in a position to tell them all to go to hell, in general, and her father in particular. That would be one reason, but another would be that brain surgery might be a way of getting to the bottom of things. She'd get all the psychiatrical training there was in the world, had most of it already, as far as that went, and back it up with an M.D. just in case; then she'd wrap it all up in a sheepskin and toss it out the window and rely wholly on her own imagination. That's the only guide. You can't know anything unless you've got the kind of hands that can feel it, unless you've got the kind of eyes that never see the outside of anything, just cut straight down under. The surface is forever a hoax, a commonplace, uninteresting thing for kids to waste time on. 'But,' she said, 'I digress. After all, this is your flask I'm holding, and this is your gin in it, and it's strictly within the law for you to have a turn, unless I wanted to be unkind and tell you that alcoholic beverage is prohibitive, pardon, prohibited, in this land, and more than that, that possession is nine points of the law even if it *is* illegal. There's an interesting point in law, or, if you wish, an interesting case in point.'

Rick took the flask and drank and handed it to her. 'Go on,' he said. There was a rough spot in her voice, and he liked to listen to it.

In college, she said, she wanted to be a writer — you know how kids always want to grow up and *be* something — fireman, engineer, interior decorator, aviator, actress? She wrote white-hot lyrics heavily inspired from Baudelaire, but always going his Pièces Condamnées one or two better. Wrong approach, I guess. But the college literary magazine wouldn't print any except the ones that were so symbolic that nobody could see through them, and the mood passed when *The Dial* gave her a blanket rejection on fifty-nine poems. Good thing, too, a very most fortunate thing to have happened, because you don't find out anything about what's true by lolling around in a girls' school writing what you think might be. You find it by going to disordered minds, looking deep into them. Disorders that result in claustrophobia in that musician or in morphinomania in the vaudeville fellow. Start with that and work back from effects to causes. Master the disorders and you're practically there. Dear God, so many things to learn, and the rain tearing down all the time.

She tilted the flask all the way up and said, 'It's empty.'

Rick set about to master the system of his overcoat, and when he had it beat he found another flask, a leather one, in a hip pocket. There you are. Be prepared, and you'll never be caught unprepared.

'There's a lot to that, you know,' she said. 'It was my guiding principle all through school, but I lost it in college some place, and now I'm never prepared.'

And while she was threading it out, letting the words weave a senseless pattern all their own, she let go the whole way and showed cause why she should hate her father; — no, not hate, you can't hate pure stupidity; yes, you can, if it's done up in a leather case of pompous, pretentious, pedantic, what-all — too bad that went down on me, she said; I really had it going there for a minute. — Hate was the word, after all. She'd hated her father in a nice neat way ever since her mother did away with herself. He was, her father was, a doctor in Cleveland, one of those stupid country doctors that doesn't know a speculum from a stethoscope, but he had a tremendous practice and he was well thought of in the profession, as thoughts go in the profession. Her mother, as she remembered her, was something else again, something pretty wonderful. '— I used to go completely to pieces when she told me my handwriting was improving, I thought so highly of that lady. — Funny, when I think about her now all I can get is that she smelled like something I've never been able to find since. I've sniffed perfume stoppers until I was blue in the face, but I've never found it.' And when Amy was twelve, this lovely lady, Amy said, started having headaches that nearly drove her mad, and that fool doctor, her husband, probably gave her aspirin if anything. At last, when he knew it was serious, he bethought himself and diagnosed the thing as a brain tumor, which it might well have been, and nobody knew but that he might have tried to cure it with a poultice. He never got anybody on the case that knew anything, and one night his wife didn't want any more of it and she jumped from the window and dropped to the forecourt of the hospital.

'Only four stories,' Amy said, 'but it did the trick.'

'Too bad.'

'You never know, I suppose,' Amy said. 'All I know is that I've been in one school or another ever since, memorizing the wrong answers. He pays the bills, but I just don't like to see him any oftener than I have to. He's married again, and what he got serves him right.'

'Good idea to put a slit in a flask,' she said almost immediately. She held it up, trying to get some light into it. 'It gives you something to go by. Your turn, Richard; drink according to your need.'

He tilted the flask up sharply, and while he drank she watched him, saying: 'Men are so much less mussy than women. There's nothing, I suppose, so really classic as a wing collar and a white tie.'

'It's almost the only kind of clothes I wear,' Rick said; 'I sleep in the day time.' He looked at her and said, 'Your turn, Doctor.'

Her eyes were wide open and clear. 'Don't call me Doctor, Richard. I've got my reasons for hating it.'

'I'm sorry,' he said. 'I won't, then.'

'It's true, though,' she said, when she had drunk from the flask; 'there's nothing in the world so beautiful and so astonishing as the spectacle of a really disordered mind. Unless,' she said after a minute, 'unless it's Josephine. Where do you suppose she is? She was here a moment ago.'

'We took her home,' Rick said. 'How do you happen to know her?'

'How does anyone happen to do anything?' Amy said. 'As far as I know, you happen to do what you happen to want to do. It's called freedom of the will, or determinism, depending on where you stand. It's simply a question of making up your mind to do what you have to do. Nothing to it. So I saw Josephine the opening night of Big Trouble, and I met her that night too. You get what you bid for.'

A car came out of a side street going fast. The taxi stopped short and the trumpet case fell off the seat. Rick laid the girl back, then, and kissed her. Her mouth was cool and firm. It was a change, something he didn't know.

'You're tired, aren't you?' he said.

She sat up and looked at him, very close to him.

'No,' she said. 'No, I'm not tired.'

'It's entirely up to you,' Rick said, very quietly, not touching her. 'I believe I love you.'

3

BEFORE the entrance of Amy North, Rick's life went along almost by appointment. He worked hard and liked it; after hours he sought out birds of his feather, and then it wasn't work and he liked it even better. He sat in with one band after another, played two pianos with Jeff Williams, played behind Josephine Jordan on recordings, and made records with who knows how many pick-up bands. He could do one thing, and that almost filled his time. For the rest, he gave himself five or six hours of deep sleep sometime during the day, he had a mild interest in the horses, a child's faith in inside straights, and the girls he knew could all be called babe. Good, straightforward life, and shaped toward the single purpose of playing a trumpet that nothing could touch.

But after the night when Amy came into Galba's with Josephine, nothing was ever the same. She shouldn't have come in; she knew too much and never understood any of it. She knew by instinct that Rick was one of the marked men, one of the odd-numbered ones. She wanted to find out what it was and why it was in him, and she must have forgotten what it was she was trying to find out about Josephine when she saw Rick, or else she must have decided that it didn't interest her any longer.

Rick didn't have a chance to know what was happening to him. It was just there, very suddenly, and nothing to do about it. He'd never known a really complicated woman, the kind who knows how to strip the nerves and kick the will around, the kind whose voice can say anything. Such a one was Amy North, the terribly good-looking one who wore too-expensive sweaters and scarcely ever got to her classes.

When she came into a room, Rick felt it and his knees went cold. When she bent her head to light a cigarette from the match he held, he was lost until the flame burned his finger. When she stood in her long white robe in front of the fireplace, propping an elbow against the mantel and crossing her feet in the classic attitude of insouciance, he couldn't let himself look at her; the sight of her twisted him.

It would have been much simpler all around if they hadn't got married. The thing would have died down, as these things do, and no harm done. But it didn't go that way. It went the hard way; ordeal by marriage.

Rick was spell-bound and reverential. He spent the night before the wedding in a Turkish bath, in the state of mind of a squire about to receive knighthood. He didn't know how it had happened, but he knew it was true, that Amy North would marry him. Most fortunate of musicians.

It's much more difficult to understand Amy's side of it than Rick's. It wasn't Amy's nature to sign her name to anything. She could talk the night out, do anything she wanted to with a word spoken, but she never put anything in writing. She was born cagey. And yet she signed the marriage license legibly and with a steady hand, and when, under oath, she said 'I do,' almost anyone would have thought she did.

Rick moved in with her. She had an apartment and she owned the andirons, the sofa, the phonograph, the pictures, and the books that were in it. All Rick had to do was to hang his clothes in a closet, give away his phonograph, and stack his records with hers. It was never Rick's house; it couldn't have been. It would have been called a studio apartment. There was a skylight across one wall of the living-room, but there the studio aspect ended, and the rest was a matter of comfort for the other half to live in.

It couldn't have been Rick's house. It is conceivable that a good salesman could have got him to buy a

Maxfield Parrish for decorative purposes, but he could never have known the painters Amy liked. She had ten or so good reproductions of French moderns on her walls. The four walls of the bedroom supported four paintings of the female nude: north, south, east, and west; Gaugin, Renoir, Cézanne, Matisse. On the wall above the mantel in the living-room there was another Matisse, the one called The Piano Lesson. When Rick looked at it for a long time one day and spelled P–L–E–Y–E–L backwards the way it was painted on the piano in the picture, Amy said, 'Yes, French for Steinway.'

There wasn't much chance, of course, for anything good to work out of it. Rick didn't know what his wife was talking about most of the time she talked. But she was well rounded; she could speak the esperanto of normal males, too, and when she did she was very good at it. She was too good at everything. She kept her Phi Beta Kappa key hanging by a chain from the head of the shower, to remind her, she said, that she was too bright a girl ever to try anything funny in the bathroom, like drowning herself standing up or drinking iodine through a straw.

The truth probably was that she married Rick because she would have given her eyes to have what he had, to have one firm ability and along with it the intimate, secure knowledge that it was worth something. She may have thought (she had her mystical side) that by marrying him she could share this depth with him, like sharing his name.

They did have a good time. They were natural spend-thrifts, both of them, and during the time they tried to act domestic, purse-strings were nothing to them. They bought a Steinway, full sized and black as a crow; they bought a down quilt covered with blue satin and marked with a white M, a quilt so light you could almost blow it around the room. The Steinway and the quilt started them, and they went from there to a deep white rug that turned out to be the wrong color to trample underfoot. Then they discovered that they were devoted to monograms and had M's put all over everything. And when all the obvious things had been bought, they felt let-down, and so they worked out on surprises for each other, things like pajamas and dressing gowns, wrist watches and pipes and gloves and cigarette cases and cologne and shirts, ties, socks, books, records, God knows what. Surprise after surprise.

At first they were together almost all the time except when Rick was actually working. They had dinner together, half the time at home, and then Amy went to a show or saw her friends or studied or killed time in her way until one o'clock when Rick was free, and then they spent the night together, sometimes around town, more often at home. The nights when they came back to the apartment and drank until nothing was

real were as close as they ever came to anything good:
the night when Amy played Stravinsky on the phonograph, and Rick, lying on the white rug in front of the
fire, swore it was Jimmy Snowden playing that trombone, nobody but Jimmy had that kind of feeling for
trombone; and the night when Rick got up and played
the piano with records to prove to Amy that he could
play the piano along with a record as easily as he could
whistle with one — if you can get a piano to trust you,
all you have to do is think what you want it to do for
you and it will. 'But they just don't like me,' Amy
said. 'Oh, I know it, they loathe me; they stiffen up
when I come near.'

'I'll tell you something,' she went on, after she'd
thought it over, 'I *can* play the piano. I know how to
play one piece, only one. It makes me feel strange to
talk about it, because once I was so in love with this
piece that it tore me all up. It was in my last year in
college and it was really driving me crazy; so I hired a
piano teacher, practically a governess, and she taught
me to play it. It took us three weeks, day and night;
and I paid that piano teacher tutor's rates and kept
her right there in my rooms.'

She stopped to light a cigarette, and then she said:
'I'll play it for you one of these times. But you can see
how it is; if you've only got one piece, you have to pick
your occasion to play it.'

The night she played it, she played it seven times.

It was Debussy, 'Clair de Lune,' and she played it impeccably. Rick had fallen asleep, and she left him and poured herself a drink and then she played it. Rick heard it far away, stood up and began to walk toward it, and when he came to the door he saw Amy across the room, her shoulders naked and white above the piano, her face tense above the music, and a long, unlighted cigarette in her mouth. The sublime grotesque. Rick stood in the doorway and let himself see her as she was. He never got over it. And that was the only time he ever heard her play.

But the nights turned up one after the other and the days followed them in natural sequence. The Martins sank below the surface and stayed there. They were crazy about each other, and crazy. They were groggy tired, too, all the time, and the pulse-beat of either one of them would have been a thing to record and think about.

In those days and on those nights Amy was peerless, She was night itself, and through it all there was her voice cool and clear as spring-water telling Rick things he had never heard, and never would understand for having heard them. She spoke words that were their own reason for being and she spoke them to hear herself speak. She would twist suddenly in Rick's arms, and of all the things she could have had to say to him then, she might say, 'God, I love Shakespeare.'

4

THE change came when Amy reformed. She was sick
one day, so very ill that Rick called a doctor. The only
thing the doctor could say was that she needed rest and
iron shots and that it might be a good idea when she
felt better to go through the clinic. When he left, Amy
roused herself enough to tell off the medical profession
once more, bunch of tramps, not one of them with
nerve enough to come clean and call a hangover a
hangover. You don't have to go to medical school to
know a hangover. You'd know a hangover, wouldn't
you, Rick?

'Oh yes, I'd know a hangover.'

'Then why did you call in that punk to tell me iron
shots and clinic?'

'If I don't have a hangover, I don't see why you do.'

'Oh, but I do,' Amy said. 'I'd know one anywhere.
I get cumulative ones every second month, and when
I get them, I want to die.'

She stayed in bed that day and night, and when Rick
came home she only said hello and went back to sleep.
She was up early the next day. She went to Columbia
and somehow got herself reinstated in her classes, had
dinner with a school friend of hers, and was asleep
when Rick came home.

She was busy and impersonal. Overnight she became
Spartan Boy, took her showers cold, and bought a

rowing machine. She went to a brain-modeling class Tuesdays and Thursdays from two to five, and to topographical anatomy at the same time Mondays and Fridays. She spent Monday, Wednesday, and Friday mornings being told about the physiology of the endocrine glands, and Tuesday and Thursday mornings she was at the Psychopathic Hospital with four internes doing clinical psychometrics. She always had dinner in town, and she was almost always asleep when Rick came in.

It had Rick worried. He was sure he'd done something wrong, but he couldn't think what. One Wednesday afternoon he got Amy cornered and asked her about it straight out. She acted professional for a minute or two, explaining patiently that she was a student, and that being a student entailed going to classes, and that study was required if one were to progress with the class work, that one's brain didn't do its best work on a regimen of straight alcohol and no sleep; ah no, it did its worst work, it did no better work than that putty brain there on the desk. She kept it going on and on; she'd got into the groove of a patient, slightly ironic way of speaking and she couldn't let it go.

Then, when there wasn't much more to say, she broke out of it suddenly and said: 'Oh, damn it, Rick, I've simply *got* to amount to something. I've got to stay with it this time. Let's have a drink and talk it over.'

There was a long talk, and Rick failed to make the only point he could honestly make, that life had been so much pleasanter before Amy went back to school; and Amy, on the other hand, made point after glorious point in defense of science, scholarship, feminism, one's debt to society, work to be done, faith, hope, charity. She had herself stirred to the core. Rick was stirred only by the feeling that he'd lost her. If she did stick it out and become a psychiatrist, it was almost certain that they'd never go shopping again. There was scarcely anything for him to say. He finished his drink, went to the piano, and played 'Blue Room' for the sadness that was in his bones. Amy stood beside her desk and poked at the lump of putty. Then she left the room, and a moment later Rick could hear the shower going full force, symbol of discipline, emblem of the great reformation. He sat at the piano and listened to the shower, and when he found himself wondering whether Amy still took showers with her watch on, he got up and left.

There was almost no chance for him to see her. When he came home at night all he could do was watch her sleep. He stopped coming home and began to wander around town, killing time until morning so that he could go back and watch her get up and go off to school. She was constantly pushing her sleeve up to look at her watch while he talked to her. She didn't seem to mind seeing him, but when she talked it was never the old, flowing, senseless talk, it was a new kind of thing, a mock-professional tone that went ravishingly with the tough, clinical manner she had worked up. She would tell him, as if he'd asked her, that medicine is a matter of trial and error, and keeping it up until you know for certain that almost everything is erroneous, but still and all, my advice to you is to try a bromo-seltzer, Mr. Martin, the moment you think it might be your old trouble. I've got to get out of here if I don't want to be twelve minutes late. Get Ramundo to fix you one.

She'd do some fast, last-minute scouting for books, purse, pen, and then she'd be out the door and gone. There were times when she would turn at the door and say, 'So long,' or 'See you around,' but more often she seemed to forget that there was anyone there to say good-bye to, and Rick would stand still and hear her go down the stairs, taking them on the run, and he'd be left alone with Ramundo, the sleek-haired, smoky-eyed Filipino boy who did what cooking there was, and answered the telephone, and took the cat out, collected all the ash trays every morning and washed them and hid them, and always seemed to be trying to make the bed at the same time Rick was trying to get into it.

And beyond that there was the cat, a Siamese cat, great confidante of Amy's, that took sensual pleasure in walking across Rick's face the moment he was asleep and never a moment before. Wonderful cat. She always knew when the bars were all the way down. She never let Rick see her, she just waited under something until he was asleep. There was something about it that unnerved him.

From almost any point of view it was an unsatisfactory life, but the worst thing about it was that nothing in it ever seemed real. Everything was foreign, Ramundo, the cat, the nudes; there was nothing except the piano that the master of the house could have the slightest confidence in. He knew now that he had never known Amy. He could remember things about her; he could remember things they'd done, but it was as if someone else had told them to him. It was impossible now to believe that he and Amy had ever had more than a speaking acquaintance. She seemed not to know he lived there. They just used the house in shifts; she got it nights and he got it days. They couldn't even fight, push each other around, call names, or resort to any of the traditional air-clearers. Rick decided fifteen times that what he wanted most to do was sock her, give her a good solid clout alongside the jaw, let her know who he was, but he couldn't do anything about it when he saw her, it wouldn't have been real. There's no satisfaction in thumbing your nose at an objectionable face on a magazine cover; the act, no matter how firm, cannot discountenance the face. Nor would Amy know she'd been socked; she was too busy, too much preoccupied.

There was only one more flash from her. She came home late one afternoon to change her clothes. Rick was in bed but awake and in a mean mood, and when she came in he began to kick his head off about how Ramundo could never get around to doing the vacuum-cleaning until he got to sleep. And another thing: that dock-tailed, Oriental, female, slant-eyed cat.

Amy was standing in front of a mirror brushing her hair, using long, rough strokes. She was tightly bound around with her long, white robe, and while she brushed her hair she looked deep into her own eyes in the mirror. But still she could talk. She didn't say a thing about the cat, but she did say that Ramundo worked hard; he was a part-time student at Columbia and he did his very best to get his work to fit in with his program, and he had her permission to do the vacuum-cleaning any time he pleased, good old Ramundo did.

'How about him doing it at night?' Rick said, 'and letting me get a little sleep?'

'No. Not night. He has to do his home-work at night. He has to do his sums.' Amy bared her teeth and looked closely at them in the mirror. Then she went on to say that never in her life, not since she'd been out of dormitories, had anyone kicked about the way she ran a house. She kept a damned fine house, and not one friend of hers but would say the same.

'I'm not a friend of yours,' Rick said, and he sat up to say it. 'I'm your husband.'

Amy put down the brush, then, and looked at her husband in the mirror. His hair hung in bright rings over his forehead, his chest was bare, and his face was flushed. She turned away from the mirror, walked slowly to the bed, and lay down by his side. Then she looked up at him, curiously, and said, 'So you are, and a stunning boy, too.'

But even after that, she couldn't have dinner with him, she had an engagement. Rick asked who, and she gave a name, just any last name, Hopwood, or Hotchkiss, or Hitchcock.

Rick came home at one o'clock again that night, but Amy didn't come in either that night or the next day, and he didn't manage to see her for three days. When he did see her he was going down the stairs on his way to work at about eight-thirty, and she was coming up with a girl and a man. She was extremely friendly; she introduced him as her husband and asked him to come on back up and have a drink. She even had a kind of prideful gleam in her eye as they talked. Rick in evening clothes had a kind of somber, youthful elegance that was impressive. He shook the man's hand, bowed to the girl, and said he couldn't go back upstairs, sorry.

The man was young and bald and he wore an overcoat with a fur collar. 'You're playing in Phil Morrison's orchestra, aren't you?' he said. 'I'm terribly sorry you can't stay with us and give us a tune.'

'Sorry,' Rick said again, and Amy walked down to

the second landing with him, telling him that that was Jay Barker, terribly rich but fun, and the girl was somebody she knew, and didn't he think it would be sort of fun if after the dance he could round up Smoke and Jeff and she'd try to catch Josephine; it would really amuse Jay to meet them, and he was crazy about jazz.

'You've been drinking,' Rick said.

'Oh, God, yes,' Amy said. 'Haven't you?'

'Yes,' said Rick, looking at her. 'I mean no.'

'I can't stay here forever,' Amy said. 'It's impolite. See you around one-thirty.'

He went on down the stairs and took a taxi to the hotel. He had a good night on the stand. He was playing for the fun of it for the first time in months; not quite for the fun of it, but for the relief of being free of Amy after all the poison she'd fed him. He was as light-hearted as a boy out of school, because he didn't have to care any longer where Amy was or what she was doing; he just didn't have to give a damn. The vision he had of those three coming up the stairs was all it took. He felt good and clear in his mind now. That punk saying give us a tune didn't even make him sore, it just made him laugh his head off. Give *who* a tune, for God's sake?

Morrison came up to him during an intermission and asked him why he was hitting so hard, had he had good news or what? Sounds like a bugle.

'Too loud?' Rick said. 'I'll play nice next time. Give me a nickel; I've got to do some phoning.'

'You can't phone now. You're on with the trio.'

'How's about Mr. C. going on with the trio? I got to phone.'

He turned away from Phil and left by a back door, no look of mutiny on his face. Phil looked at the door, gave it a look that would have split some doors, but not this door. Then he went to get a man to bat for Rick. He could have let himself get sore, but he knew better. He was a slave-driver, and pity wasn't in him, but love was. He loved his band, he loved the money it brought in, and he loved Rick Martin, first trumpet. The band leader never lived who could have stood in front of Rick night after night for all those years and not feel thankful for every phrase he played.

He found Jack Crandall and said, 'Go play for the trio. Martin's on a tear,' and Jack Crandall said, 'He's been letting it go, all right.'

'He'll pipe it down,' Morrison said. 'I just spoke to him.'

Rick telephoned The Afrique too late to catch Smoke in an intermission, but he left a message: 'This is Martin. *Rick* Martin. Tell Mr. Jordan I'll pick him up after the show and we'll go over the line down to Silver's if he wants to. Tell him to ask anybody else he wants and I'll try to get some guys myself. Tell him I'll get a car and he can bring the potato salad, and if he can't

go have him call me before one. Is that straight?
Before one here. Tell him I'll bring Barrow if I can
get him. I'd have called sooner only I just got the idea.
Any time before one.'

He made three more calls, invitations to get in it.
He slipped into his chair at the exact moment Morrison
was ready to start the next set, and he played himself
back into good repute in no time at all.

At one when they were clearing away, Phil came up
and said he hoped he wasn't sore about anything and
that he hoped he wouldn't forget overnight that they
were making a record tomorrow at ten.

'I'll be there,' Rick said. 'I'm making one at eleven
behind Josie Jordan, too.'

'Did you ever sit in with the U.S. Army band on a
record?' Morrison said. 'There's a bet you missed.'

'They might ask me yet,' Rick said.

He left and took the biggest Chrysler they had at the
U-Drive Garage. Milt Barrow was standing on the
curb in front of The Afrique, and Les Cohen was with
him. They had their instrument cases tucked under
their arms and their shoulders were hunched under their
collars. It was a cold night. Rick pulled the car into
the sidewalk and one wheel jumped the curb. Barrow
and Cohen scattered for cover, and didn't come out
from behind a lamp post and a mail box until Rick had
killed the engine trying to get the car back on the street.

'Where did you *get* that car?' Barrow said

'I bought it,' Rick said with pride, 'and it's a dinger. Get some of this.' He got out and fiddled around with a spotlight mounted on the running board — a big light, almost two feet across. It came on and sent out a beam that stayed strong and round for five hundred feet.

'They use this one when they've got to drum up trade at the Paramount. Is that a light!' He stood behind it on the running board and turned it straight up in the air.

'Look at that old light *go*,' he said. 'I start flashing this light around in windows and I bet guys would start jumping out, one after another.'

'This is the same car you had last year the night we went up to New Rochelle; I know this one.'

'This is the one I always buy.'

'Turn it off. You got to have a permit to run a light around like that.'

'No you don't.' Rick shot the beam straight into a window of The Afrique, and then snapped the light off. 'That'll make them think twice in there,' he said. 'Let's go in. Freeze our feet off out here.'

They met Smoke and Jeff and Hazard coming out.

'Where'd you get the car?' Smoke said.

'It's a U-Drive,' Rick said.

'What's the idea of you driving it up on the side-walk?'

'Oh, I don't know. I was going to stop it right there

by the curb, but I couldn't get the cock-eyed thing to
quit moving. Something went haywire, I guess.'

'Who's going to drive it?' Smoke said, looking at
it.

'I am,' Rick said. 'I'm a damn good driver, once I
get the hang of it. It just takes me a little while to get
onto it after all this time.' He looked at Smoke, who
was kicking a tire to see if it was still all right. 'Unless
you'd like to,' he said. 'You can drive it if you want to.'

Smoke got in under the wheel, saying, 'Well, I sort
of would like to.'

They drove through the tube and five miles into New
Jersey to a road-house off the highway, a place known
as Silver's. Silver's was always the first place the law
looked into when a round-up was called, but that didn't
hurt business any. A woman named Olga Vogel ran it;
it was called Silver's for someone no longer there.

The three white ones and the three black ones
stomped into the house and got a greeting. The players
are come to Elsinore and they're of a mind to play.
'Lookit the jig-men,' Olga said. 'I thought you'd give
us the go-by. How are you, Rick Martin? Hi, Art;
Hi, Jeff, Smoke, Miltyboy. Who's your little friend
here? So? A Mr. Cohen? Glad to see you, Mr. Cohen;
there's always room here for a countryman. You boys
want to stay down here, or do you want to be alone?
There's a piano both places.'

'We don't want to play,' Smoke said. He had drums

hanging all over him. 'We just come out to see how everything's getting along out here.'

'You'd better go upstairs,' Olga said. 'Lou Marble's up there. She was singing awhile ago. I don't know what she's doing now.'

Olga pushed them through the room and into a door that opened on some stairs. Rick was the last one, and she linked an arm through his on the way upstairs.

'They tell me you married a society girl, Rick,' she said. 'Is she pretty?'

'No,' Rick said, 'she looks like a coal miner.'

'What's her name?' Olga said.

'North.'

'Sort of an odd name for a girl, isn't it?'

They went into a big room. There was a fireplace at one end of it and a bar at the other and ten or fifteen empty tables scattered around.

'Name it and take it,' Olga said at the bar. 'This one's on the house.'

They named it. Gin straight down the line. Six golden fizzes.

Olga said, 'My God, not only do I set up drinks but also a half-dozen eggs. Why don't you ever come out any more?' she said to Art Hazard. 'Did I do something to annoy you boys?'

'You didn't annoy me,' Art said. 'Rick got married, and none of us seen anything of him. And anyhow it's been too cold to get out of town. You say Lou Marble was here? I don't see anything even looks like her in here.'

'She left,' the barman said. 'She got sick and her friend took her out back.'

Rick was at the end of the line, next to Jeff, saying: 'We'd just call it the barrelhouse eight or some name, and we could make records that would split them all wide open, make them sit up. Do up a lot of old ones, "Twelfth Street Rag," "China Boy," "Dinah," "Lime-house," "Bugle Call," all the ones we used to play; make a regular thing of it, same bunch all the time under the same name.'

'They wouldn't do it,' Jeff said. 'No record company would want it, because it wouldn't sell enough records. The only records that pay for themselves are the new ones with a vocal. People buy them to learn the words.'

'We could get Josie in and give them vocals, or else Cromwell from Morrison's; he knows how to sing.'

'Yah, but they already know the words to the old ones. They buy records to learn new words. They don't care how you play it. You and Art on the same record wouldn't matter a damn to more than two hundred people in the whole country. Who buys records is the high-school girls. You know that? Talk to that man Brown and he'll tell you. I had the same idea myself once. But the really good stuff doesn't sell records. Oh, in two three years it does, but they don't like to wait that long. They like to make them and sell them the same day. Guys that gang around music stores to buy Morrison's records as soon as they're released get to hear some damned good horn playing, but they don't know it. They just want to learn the words.'

'I never thought of it that way,' Rick said. He drank with a sad look on his face.

'It's the true,' Jeff said. 'Nobody knows what we're doing but us, the guys that do it. I've heard them say they liked our record of "Melancholy Baby," and I say thanks, what did you like about it? and they say it's sort of catchy or some damn thing. And that's about the best record we ever made, some ways. The way Jimmy slides out of Davis's solo there and runs up eight bars enough to drive a man crazy, best piece of trambone playing I ever heard in my life, absolutely the best piece of trambone, and they say catchy; cute tune. I never heard anybody except you and two or three others even mention Jimmy on that record. That man Brown at the studio never even heard it, and he was there when we made the record. It's a long time ago now, but with Jimmy playing like that I think it's maybe our best record.'

There was depth in his voice. He was talking about the thing, not the people.

'Hell,' Rick said, 'maybe we're all lucky to have jobs, one way you look at it. Maybe we're lucky to get tunes like "Melancholy Baby" that get so popular they'll sell no matter how good you play them.'

'We couldn't sell "Twelfth Street," or "Dinah," all over again, I know that, if we had Gabriel himself sitting in,' Jeff said, 'unless we had the money to do it on our own hook, pay the cost ourselves.'

'What would it cost?'

'Plenty; more than we could get together in ten years.'

'Maybe we could get some rich bastard that likes good jazz to stake us.'

'*You* get him.'

'I guess you're right,' Rick said. 'Let's go sit down.'

They broke away from the line at the bar and sat down at a table. They were something to look at, the two of them there: Jeff, the thoughtful, the Latin-featured, and Rick, the tight-drawn Northman, saying what they thought, knowing that art is long and life is a moment.

'If we'd just get a good bunch together, though,' Rick said one more time, 'get Barrow to play sax, and this kid Cohen I brought tonight, and La Porte that plays fiddle for Morrison, he can play it really *hard*, so that it sounds as good as any instrument in the band. Funny thing, you should have heard him up at Jameson's one night; you wouldn't think a man could do that with nothing but a fiddle, but he sure was. It was just as *hard*, just as ... I don't know; he's *good*, that's all; you wouldn't think a damned old vi'lin ...'

'I know it,' Jeff said. 'I heard him on the record he

was in with Deane's. He's the best thing on the record. It doesn't matter so much what a man plays, if he knows how. Take whatshisname, guy that plays the marimba at Moss's ...'

'Roland.'

'Yeah. The way he plays it it sounds like a piano, only different, better than a piano. And there's nothing I hate, usually, like a marimba.'

'Me too,' Rick said. 'I can smell them a mile. And then here's this boy Roland, that knows something to do to it, and I get so I really *like* the thing.'

'Ain't it the truth? Same way with me. Remember in "Muddy Water" the way he comes in there, three notes over and over like he can't get off it, and then it breaks over and he's going, remember? Goes sort of like this.'

Jeff got up and went to the piano, hit a note or two, and then sat down and played single notes with his right hand as if he were hammering them out. Rick went over and watched him.

'That's it,' he said. 'That sounds exactly like it. It sounds like a piano all right; I mean you make it sound like that marimba.'

He opened his trumpet case, wiped off his trumpet and put the mouthpiece in, and stood there a minute listening to Jeff before he began to play. Then they were playing 'Muddy Water' and Rick was driving it straight ahead, not doing anything in particular, just playing the simple tune one note after the other, and making each single note a shining, fresh thing. He stopped at the end of one chorus, and Jeff took it while he listened, and when Jeff's chorus was complete, he tilted his trumpet up and took his turn, fulfilling the promise that was in the restraint of his first playing. Jeff looked up at him, squinting his eyes to give more knowledge to his ears. The four men at the bar turned around and listened, their heads twisted sharply up for the sound. It was pure Martin, unmistakable. He stood, one foot hooked over the rung of a chair, and he blew the breath of life into that lean, whip-like trumpet.

The four at the bar drifted up toward him, and Olga stayed where she was, leaning against the bar smoking a brown cigarette. Smoke pulled a couple of metal tubes out of his vest pocket, shot the brushes out of them, and began to drum lightly against the sides of his legs. Les Cohen's eyes were popped out a little watching Rick, and every little while he'd shake his head and whisper boy. He was only nineteen then, and it was the first time he'd ever been asked out with any of the great ones.

Rick stopped playing, drew his sleeve across his mouth, and said, 'I thought we were going to do some drinking.' He put the trumpet on top of the piano and went to the bar, but the others didn't follow; they found their cases and got ready to play.

Rick came back with a glass for Jeff and set it on the piano — can't be playing piano around here on mush

and milk, try this one. You like that? Pink; it's got
grenadine in it; I'd better ask the General over there
to make us up a bowl of this and put it where we can
get to it easy. He went back to the bar and asked
and it was done. A full pitcher of it, pink lemonade
of a sort. Rick drank a tumbler full of it at a shot,
just as a thirst-quencher. Playing made him thirsty.
It burns a man to tear music out of himself for a long
time; it dries him out, leaves salt in his mouth, dust in
his throat. He has to keep it wetted down, keep everything moving easily, not let anything grate against
anything else.

— General, fill up the jug, but not with any more of
that pink wash; fill it up, dear General, with some of
that French cognac out of the bottle with the stars
on it.

They played music, then; piano, drums, two reeds,
two brass. Smoke marked out the boundaries for them
and led them wherever they went with a beat that pulled
them along, a sensitive, infinitely various, but uncom-
promising beat — the core, the pumping heart of music.

It was an all-star show that night at Silver's. The
only unproven man in it was young Les Cohen, and he
proved himself twenty times before the night was out,
playing a clarinet that was a wild, sweet thing. He had
them raising their eyebrows at each other.

'When'd you start playing that clair'net?' Smoke
said to him, and Les said:

'Oh, papa took it on a loan and the guy never paid, and I got to blowing around on it so much that papa got me a teacher for a couple of weeks. I guess I was twelve.'

'You'd be sure out of luck if the guy'd come back and pay up now, and take it away, now you've put yourself to so much trouble learning how to play it,' Milt Barrow said.

'That would be all right,' Les said. 'I'd just go and buy another one.'

'You would? Well, ain't you the kid, though!'

'What are you guys doing, trying to kid me?' Les said. The liquor and the excitement had him pretty vague.

Rick said, 'You play that clarinet of yours, boy, and none of them can kid you; nobody in the band business can tell you anything when you're playing that thing that way, don't you know that?'

The boy blushed all the way up, and Rick poured him another drink. 'Here, toss that down and see if you can do any worse or better.'

He looked across at Art Hazard, that great black ball bouncing on the edge of a little chair. 'What would you care to play now, Mr. Hazard?'

'I don't care much *what* we play, Mr. Martin,' Art said, 'just so we get playing it while I can still hold on to this here iron horn of mine. Keeps slipping out of my hand like nobody's business. I don't know what's ailing it tonight.'

'Funny,' Rick said. 'I've got just the other trouble. I can't seem to keep mine from sticking to my hand. Can't shake it off. Like that damned cat.'

'What damned cat?'

'Oh, just a damned cat. Keeps walking on my face, sticking to my hand.'

'I used to know a guy that got toads,' Hazard said. 'They'd hop all over his bed, hop all over everything. Hop hop. He tried to stab one once and got himself in the leg, right in the shin. Never did heal up.'

'But this cat,' Rick said, 'I've really got this cat. It sort of belongs to me. It's a Siamese cat, and they're the worst kind.'

'So did this other guy I was telling you about. He was in bad shape with those toads.'

'But this cat — oh hell...' Rick picked up his trumpet and played the opening bars of "Bugle Call" good and loud, and the rest of them were ready for it with a terrific blare at the end of the opening bars; they kicked it back and forth among them, twenty choruses, taking turns at solo variations on the actual bugle call and then jamming through the rest of the thing all together; then reversing the process and doing the bugle call all together and laying off and letting one man solo it through to the end, which was never the end but simply a return to the bugle call. Never-ending bugle call; endless belt of bugle call.

They played hard and they played well and it wasn't

all solo either. Toward daylight they had built up a
blend of melody and harmony that was older and
emotionally deeper than the brave virtuosity of the
first hours. It was the music of men who look backward with wisdom rather than forward with faith.
They were tired now, and dependent on each other,
not so ruggedly individualistic. They brought the
dawn in with sad and mellow music.

> Woke up this morning when chickens were crowing for day,
> And on the right side of my pillow my man had gone away.

'What time's it getting to be?' Milt said, and Rick
looked at his watch, but he couldn't make much of it,
it moved too fast for him. He looked at it, held it this
way, held it that way, and then he knew that something was wrong. He felt waves of intense heat come
up his spine and rise to his head, one after the other,
and he tried to get his coat off, but then it was all over
and he was on the floor with Smoke and Jeff bending
over him and telling each other to go get some water.
Their faces came into focus and he sat up and looked
around.

'I remember falling off the chair,' he said, 'just as
plain. I was sitting there looking at my watch; then I
was falling and falling; it felt like a mile.'

'It wasn't no mile,' Smoke said, as if to a child; 'it
was only from there to there. Get up. You're all
right.'

'Sure,' Rick said. 'All I need is a drink. And not

any of that fancy French dope, either. What I need is some liquor.'

He got up, made a pass at his knees, put his hand on Smoke's shoulder, and they walked to the bar, which was no longer attended by a keeper. Smoke smelled at two or three bottles, and then poured three fingers of whisky into a tumbler and shoved it at Rick.

'Drink that,' he said, 'and lay off this faintin. Scared the pants off me.'

'Me too,' Rick said. 'Did I say anything? I mean, like talking in your sleep?'

'No, nothing. You didn't say anything until you sat up.'

'What did I say then?'

'You said you fell down.'

Rick drank the drink, and all the rest of them came up to the bar and helped finish the bottle and told what they knew about fainting. — Fainting's the same thing as passing out, only shorter; you pass out, you're out for quite a while generally. It's like sleeping when you can't wake up. Fainting's different; you go under a minute and then you come up again.

'It's a hell of a silly feeling,' Rick said. 'You can't help what you're doing.' He poured a half-inch of whisky into his glass and drank it. 'I've got to get back to town,' he said. 'Morrison's making a record at ten. What time is it now?'

Eight-fifteen, broad daylight and time to be getting

out of New Jersey. 'Get your stuff and let's go,' Rick said. 'What happened to my horn when I took the fall? Anybody see it?'

'Yes,' Milt Barrow said. 'It bounced on the floor and lit on top of the piano.'

'It's all right,' Les Cohen said. 'I'll get it for you.'

He brought the trumpet and handed it to Rick, and Rick looked it over, pushed the valves, ran up the scale light as a feather, went through some arpeggios, and handed it back to Cohen. 'Thanks,' he said. 'Put it away, will you?'

All of them went to get their coats and cases then, and Smoke stayed with Rick at the bar. Rick took a bill out of his wallet and put it on the counter under the empty bottle — leave that there for Olga and the General.

'That's a lot of money,' Smoke said. 'You got anything smaller?'

'Oh, what the hell? Cost us more than that to hire a hall, and we had this to ourselves all night.'

'Hire ten halls for that.'

'Olga thought we were sore. Let her know we aren't. I like Olga.' He sagged against the bar, saying: 'I've got to keep going everywhere telling everybody I'm not sore all the time. I got to keep doing that until I tell all of them. Stay away a night or two and they think you're high-hatting them.'

'You been away longer than a night or two,' Smoke

said, 'but nobody thinks you're stuck up; they all
know you got married, that's all. Get married you got
to stay home more, that's all. That's why Arnold
started that cigar store, and got out of music; he had
to get out. It can happen to anybody. That's just
some guys' nature, is all.'

Rick looked up and said: 'Trouble with you, you
talk too damn much. Pop off about everything. What
do you know about some guys' nature, for Christ's
sake?'

Smoke gulped and looked startled. His voice was
sad. 'I don't know,' he said. 'I was just thinking about
when Arnold left the band. He told me he never got
any time to see his children, and his wife got to worrying
him, and he just figured he could buy this store and be
around home nights, like other guys. I was just telling
you. Just thought I'd tell you about Arnold.'

'Oh, all right; tell me about him.'

'I did. Already.'

'Good. But listen, you. I'm not ready to run
nobody's cigar store, yet. And I'm not sticking around
home. And I wouldn't marry the best bitch ever stepped
in shoe leather, and don't forget it.'

'You already did.'

'Her? Well, what if I did, what about it, it hasn't
made me any different, has it? Just because I wasn't
around much for a while, do I get corny? Did I look
bad tonight?'

'Baby, you never looked better in your life.'

'Well, lay off me, then. Let me alone; quit ragging me, for God's sake. I've got to figure something out, only I can't when you keep shooting off your mouth about cigar stores every minute. I got to figure something out.'

He pitched forward a little and Smoke caught him and leaned him back against the bar.

'You're all right, boy,' Smoke said. 'Come on, let's go in and run some water over our heads before we go back to town.'

He took Rick's arm, and Rick said, 'You're the only friend I've got, only guy cares whether I live or die, aren't you?' And Smoke said: 'Everybody does. No, not there. In here.'

Smoke turned on a tap and held Rick's head under it for two or three minutes. Every time Rick began to bridle, Smoke would apply the pressure of his hand on the back of his neck a little more firmly, but always smoothly, no violence. He kept him under the tap as long as he wanted him to stay; there were no two ways about this business. It was a measure, not a pleasure.

The iron hand slackened, and Rick stood up and shook his head and threw water all over the place and all over Smoke.

'Just like giving a dog a bath to try fixing you up,' Smoke said. 'Only *you* could have told me you was

going to shake. I might as well go in myself, now.' He
turned on the tap and pushed his head into the stream.
Not a towel in the place. They dried their necks with
their handkerchiefs and just let the water drip off their
heads.

'Good thing I did that,' Rick said on the way out.
'I wasn't feeling so good for a minute or two back there.
Where the guys?'

They were in the car waiting, looking cold. Rick got
in under the wheel and Smoke got in from the same
side and shoved him over and started the car himself.
Rick asked politely what the idea was, and Smoke said
no idea, he just thought he'd drive. Just felt like it,
somehow; you know how sometimes you get to feeling
like one thing or another?

Les Cohen was on the other side of Rick. Halfway
into New York he fell asleep, his head bent back over
the back of the seat, and Rick said how that boy could
sleep driving along in that kind of weather beat him.
Must be five ten degrees below zero. And having said
the words he went into a chill, a real one. His teeth
chattered, bone against bone, and he shook all over.
He tried to light a cigarette for warmth, but he couldn't
make it, and Barrow lighted it for him and stuck it in
his mouth. But that didn't do any good; the cigarette
dropped out of his mouth in the next spasm of shaking,
and he burned his hand trying to find it. It was a bad
ride. When they were back in town they took Les and

Barrow and Art home and then it was ten minutes to ten, and the three of them went to the Grandbranch Building without stopping for breakfast or a change of clothes.

Morrison and most of his band were in the studio when Rick and Smoke and Jeff came in. It made a stir: Rick, hatless, his hair stiff all over his head in frozen curls, his face pearl-gray with no light in it. There were ashes all over the front of his overcoat, and one wing of his collar had pulled loose from the collar button and was flying free.

'How are you, Phil?' Rick said. 'Turned cold, didn't it?'

'Oh, sure, it turned cold, all right. You going to be all right to play?'

'Me?' Rick said. He took off his overcoat and dropped it on a chair. His collar poked him in the chin and he buttoned it and looked better, but not so very much.

'What happened?' Phil said to Jeff. 'Did he fall in a river?'

Smoke made the answer: 'No,' he said, 'it's just rain. What are you making this time?'

'Four sides,' Phil said. '"It Had to Be You" and " I Wonder What's Become of Joe," and then "Wistful and Blue" and "I Must Have That Man."' He kept his eye on Rick while he talked. 'We changed the arrangement on "It Had to Be You" this morning,' he said to Rick. 'The trio sings first, the way it used to be, but you come out of them and take the first full solo.'

'Good.'

The technical men were getting things ready. The studio was full of men tuning instruments, running the scale, playing snatches.

'Sit down,' Phil yelled. 'Get in your places. We're going to begin. Pull the piano up closer.' He gave directions like a section boss, told them just what to do. He always told them just what to do, because he was always the one who knew. 'You stand up there all the time,' he said to Rick. 'Stand right beside Harry and play straight into it through your chorus, and pipe down for the backgrounds.'

'Yes, Mr. Morrison,' Rick said, and he took his place beside Harry Cromwell, the hot man of the vocal trio. Smoke and Jeff sat down in a corner.

The light came on. Phil Morrison waved his stick and the trio started to sing, backed only by piano and drums, and at the end of their chorus Rick broke through, out in front of the full orchestra for a chorus that was as reckless a piece of trumpet playing as any the Grandbranch Building ever contained. He was Orpheus on the loose for thirty-two bars. At one point Smoke couldn't contain himself: he said Oh Oh right out loud, and you can still hear it on the record, if you listen closely. At the end of the solo Rick dropped back for the saxophone figures and worked in the background, but after that he couldn't be heard at all; he kept his trumpet up to his mouth but he didn't play.

He looked fine on 'Wistful and Blue,' not so mad, not so rash, but better, somehow, more intelligent and sensitive. It was the best record Morrison ever put out — a good melody, arranged not as a succession of solo choruses with varied rhythmic accompaniments, but as a beautifully developed series of variations on a clean tune. It began with a brief ensemble introduction, followed by an equally brief passage from Rick's trumpet; and the rest was a matter of fine balance, one instrument coming up to show against the background and then dropping back to let another one in. It was a pretty performance on all sides.

They didn't finish the four tunes until ten minutes after eleven, and when they opened the door, Josephine Jordan was waiting in the hall with Matthew Brown, and she was on the point of getting temperamental.

'What's the good of using another studio?' she was saying. 'What's the good of using another room, when all my accompanying artists are in here, in this one, making records for Phil Morrison?'

Smoke went toward her. 'We ain't making a record, honey,' he said; 'we're just listening to Rick make one.'

And then Josephine, who was as big a name as New York could offer in that season, wanted to know just why in hell was it that her accompanying artists would rather loll around listening to a bunch of mugs making a record than make one themselves. Which thing, she wanted to know, was more important? She tapped a patent-leather slipper, fast, while waiting for her answer. Her head was up and there was fire in her eye.

'How could we be on time to make a record with you, when Rick's going to play on it too and he had to make four for Morrison first? That's why. We're just waiting around for Rick to get through with this one, so he can work on yours.'

That brought a snort but nothing else. Rick came up to them with his trumpet under his arm. Josephine looked at him. She was open-mouthed with surprise for a moment, and then she broke into the Jordan laugh, a well-tempered version of the old Hi-Yi.

'Wait till Amy gets a look at that shiner!' Rick felt the side of his face. There was a lump on his temple where he'd struck it when he fainted.

'No shiner; it's a bump. I was in an accident.'

'Yah,' Jeff said, 'he was in an accident. It was almost pretty bad.'

'Looks bad enough to me the way it is,' Josephine said. 'It looks terrible. What are you going to tell Amy? She was burnt up anyway the way you ran out on her party last night.'

'I didn't run out. I just didn't show up. You go?'

'Sure thing, I went. You missed something, running out that way. That boy Jay's a kick; you want to watch him.'

'Who else was there?'

Nobody else, according to Josephine. Nobody else except Jay and Amy and that girl Maude, Amy's friend. Maude Petersen, enough like Amy to be her twin — walked like Amy, talked like Amy, dressed like Amy. The only difference was that Maude, if you wanted Josephine's opinion, was a little off in the head, just slightly off her nut. She'd sit and stare and stare and then say she was a negro-what's-it, a negrophile, said it twenty times, couldn't seem to get it off her mind.

'And if she's any part, I'm a Hindu,' Josephine said. 'Do you know her?'

'No,' Rick said. 'I've only heard her name.'

'She's all right, but whatever she's got it's got her worried, poor devil. She'd keep telling me she's one of these. Nothing *I* could do about it, give her another drink. She got pretty tight. We all did.'

'How was Amy?'

'Swell, same as always. Sore at you, though. She was counting on you to bring Dan and Jeff and have them play. She said you said you would. I think she was pretty sort of put out.'

'We played somewhere else,' Rick said. 'What are we going to make?'

'I told you twice last week. "Mama Goes Where Papa Goes," and "Sam, the Old Accordion Man."'

'Nice pair,' Rick said. 'It ought to sell.'

Morrison's boys were getting out; the studio was

almost empty. Phil came up to Rick and told him to get some beefsteak on that as soon as he could.

'Don't he look like hell, for a fact?' Josephine said. 'Dan and Jeff look all right, but look at *him!*'

'All three of them look like hell to me,' Phil said, and he meant it. He turned back to Rick and said, 'Another thing, they want me to make up a band for a college shindig in Boston next Friday night and they want you in it.'

'Too far,' Rick said. 'I wouldn't go to Boston if they gave it to me.'

'That's what I told them, but they won't take anybody but you, and they seemed to want you bad. Two hundred and a quarter.'

'I'll have to think it over,' Rick said. 'Boston's a hell of a ways. Tell them to have it down here and I'll play. I like to stay in town.'

'They want you there. Two and a quarter and transportation.'

'I'll think.'

Phil started to leave, but he turned at the door to come back and say, 'Get your hair cut, too; you look like a Greek.'

It was almost eleven-thirty. Rick looked at his trumpet, Josephine took off her coat, and Jeff sat down at the piano. Smoke began to assemble his drums and the four of them got their signals together: for ' Sam, the Old Accordion Man,' it was to be a lead-off by Jeff, then verse with voice, piano and drums, then chorus with Rick playing a running obbligato, then trumpet solo for the first section of the second chorus with Josephine coming in at the mid-section to finish it up. It was the stock arrangement for vocal records. Same thing for 'Mama Goes Where Papa Goes' except for trumpet in the lead-off and two bars of vamp-till-ready to build up Josephine's entrance.

Everything was set. The light came on and they started with Sam. Josephine was in form; she was always in form, anytime, day or night. Her voice was rich and rough singing

> He plays those chords like nobody can.
> They call him Sam, the old accordion man.

Rick stood right beside her and played obliquely out from every note she sang. Among them, they made a good thing of it, Josephine and Rick lifting the melody and Smoke and Jeff weaving it tight with rhythm. Josephine came through in the fine wild way she had; she was the star, it was her record, but Rick could never play anything without lighting up a little on his own.

They did Mama Goes next, and it was in that one that the unheard-of happened. It went beautifully almost to the end. Josephine sang verse and chorus, Rick played the first eight bars of the second chorus, Josephine took it from there, and then, for a finish, they went into half-time together for a short coda that built up from the tonic note higher and higher and

wilder and wilder until Josephine held it and Rick
pushed it on, staggered up and down the scale with it
until he hit his note, and then slid up to catch it once
and for all — and he fluffed. No doubt about it, it went
wrong. It would have been a killer, but it missed.

Nobody said a word. Rick held onto his trumpet
and stared straight ahead of him. Smoke and Jeff got
up and moved a step or two toward him and stopped.
Then he raised his arm and they had to grab him to
keep him from throwing the horn against the wall.
Smoke took it away from him, and he sank into a chair,
put his hands over his face, and stayed there that way.

'The record's all right,' Jeff said to him, quietly.
'They can polish off those last ribs, nothing to it.'

Matthew Brown said, 'Of course.'

Smoke put the trumpet in the case, got Rick's coat
and his own and said, 'Let's get out. We're through,'
and when Rick just sat there without moving, Josephine
leaned down and kissed him lightly on the side of the
head. 'Go ahead, baby lamb,' she said, 'and get some
steak for that. The record's wonderful.'

Rick stood up, felt in his pockets until he found a
cigarette, and lighted it. He took his coat from Smoke,
put it on, took his trumpet case, and went out the
door without saying anything.

'Whyn't you go with him?' Jeff said to Smoke.

'He don't want me; I can tell.'

Jeff and Smoke and Josephine and Matthew Brown

stood around for a while, thinking about it, and then Jeff said: 'He hasn't got any call to take it so hard. We can do it over.'

They waited a minute, and Jeff went on almost as if he were talking to himself: 'I don't know what the hell that boy thinks a trumpet will do. That note he was going for, that thing he was trying for — there isn't any such thing. Not on a horn.'

5

WORD gets around. Smoke and Jeff didn't say anything, but Josephine was female and Matthew Brown was there, and within a week it was all over town that Rick Martin had spoiled a record for Josie Jordan.

Narration varies with the narrators. The thing began, no doubt, with Matthew Brown telling someone that the record had to be scrapped, or with Josephine telling someone that Rick ran out on his wife's party and turned up next day at the studio with a blue eye. Simple statements, but a simple statement that runs the gauntlet can take a serious beating. All kinds of things were said, but the essence of all the tales was that the great Rick Martin was played out, the skids were under him, it wouldn't be long now; too bad, too; he used to be the fair-haired boy of lot until he got to tearing around with the Harlem crowd. Niggers can stand that stuff, but a white man can't.

There was a variant that started the same way but

ended by laying the blame on his having married a rich society girl and having gone soft on her old man's money. Poor bastard, he was all set to climb into the social register when the girl threw him out on his ear.

No one ever said that he was the one that did the leaving, that he left the girl because he knew, without even thinking the words, that she wasn't good enough for him. That wouldn't have occurred to anyone. And it didn't occur to anyone that the reason he stayed with the Harlem crowd was that they were his rightful friends, they were closer to the music than any of the white men were; they were close to it in the same way he was.

And finally it never occurred to anyone that he really wasn't slipping, he wasn't played out; he was only getting so good that he couldn't contain it. Nobody but Jeff Williams realized why he'd mugged up the record.

6

THERE wasn't much fuss about his leaving Amy. She was in trouble of her own and she scarcely knew when it happened. The morning Rick went back to the apartment to get his clothes, a week or so after the session at Silver's, he found her asleep on the sofa with her coat on. He'd gone in thinking she'd be away at school, but there she was asleep in the living-room with a long green dress on, and silver sandals, and a fur coat, and she started up, scared, when he came in.

'Oh, you,' she said. She didn't ask him where he'd been; he didn't ask her where she'd been. She looked around for something to say, and said: 'You'll have to pardon the condition of the house. Ramundo's taking finals.'

He looked down at her for a moment. She looked tired out.

'Don't you go to school any more?' he said.

'Me?' she said, surprised. 'Oh, yes, I go to school; I was just on my way now.'

It was all right. Neither of them cared what either of them said. It was simply a question of holding up the exterior, making speech and gesture to prove that they were of this world, human beings on the face of the earth.

'I'd like to get some things,' Rick said.

'Right,' Amy said, and he went into the hall and came back with six suits and dumped them on a chair and went out the front door and came back in five minutes with a taxi-driver. 'Those,' he said, and the driver picked up the suits and took them out. Rick went back to the hall and brought out other suits and overcoats and hats and shoes, and the driver came back and took them, while Rick packed a bag of shirts and socks and those things. Amy didn't get up from the sofa all the while he was there. She just lay there looking tired and glazed and beautiful.

When Rick came back into the studio with his bag,

she said, 'It didn't work out, did it?' 'What?' Rick said, and she said: 'The thing with us. It *was* a flop, wasn't it?'

Rick stood by a moment, not looking at her, and then he said, 'Yes, something was wrong.'

'Yes,' Amy said. 'Something always seems to be. Get your records before you tell me good-bye.'

'Keep them. I don't need them.'

'Neither do I.' Amy turned and looked up at him, with the old, curious look. 'Kiss me before you go,' she said.

Rick bent down and kissed her, but even so he left.

7

IT WASN'T so simple when he left Phil, because Phil didn't want him to go, and he really didn't want to go either. It was just one of those false plays, and it got out of both their hands, so that what happened was that Phil fired Rick and Rick quit at the same moment. Phil only meant to ask him if he didn't want to take a vacation, get some rest, but he had a nasty nature, and first thing he knew he was telling Rick either to quit drinking on the job or get out. And Rick, who had built up a taste for adulation and had never even smelled any criticism, flared like a torch and asked what it was, anyhow, a Salvation Army Band? Then he liked the sound of that and he went on to say that, come to think of it, it did sound like one; it was a foul band, a terrible band, and no wonder he got tight on the stand, sitting in there listening to it every night of his life. Either get tight or go nuts.

'So my band's foul?' Phil said.

'It's terrible,' Rick said. 'It's awful. Who've you got besides me? The trio's good, but they can't sing *all* the time. If you had enough ear to hear Jeff Williams's band just once, you'd shoot yourself.'

'I'd shoot myself on account of Jeff Williams's band! Listen, you!' Phil had his coat halfway off, but Rick simply turned around and walked out as straight as he could.

And that split a combination that had seemed as solid as the earth. Phil Morrison's Orchestra with Rick Martin, first trumpet. Mention Morrison's Orchestra in those days and you immediately thought of Rick Martin. Mention Rick Martin and you thought of his horn in Morrison's records. It had lasted five years, and that's long.

It was the first time Rick had been out of a job since the truant officer caught up with him at Gandy's. He could have had fifty jobs the first day, but he didn't want even one job. His job with Phil Morrison had been a tie with the world, like his job at Gandy's, and the moment he was free of it, he knew he didn't want any more of it. By that time, the fewer obligations he had, the better he liked it. Music, for him, wasn't a business; it was a passion, and he was ready to give up to it.

The upstairs and downstairs places saw a lot of him after he left Morrison. He made records with anybody that asked him, but he didn't sit behind any orchestra leaders and he didn't play any more hotel dance music. He simply didn't take offers. He stayed in the joints with his own kind, the incurables, the boys who felt the itch to discover something. He stayed within the closed circle of the fanatics, the old bunch of alchemists, and there he did his work. One night after another he soaked out the real world with alcohol and, free of it, he played music that could stand up with any music. There were times when a bell rang and he had the pleasure of knowing he was a good man. He knew it once in awhile. The rest of them knew it all the time, every time he played that horn.

When he stopped working for Morrison he stopped making any bones about drinking. It was all the time and nothing to do about it, no reason to have to do anything about it. Drinking was as much of a method as any he'd ever worked out, and it served two purposes for him: it gave him a way out, a means of pushing out beyond the actual, banal here-and-now, and at the same time it kept him on his feet. Something had to keep him on his feet; he was tired in those days, dog-tired all the time, ready to drop. If he'd ever unwound and relaxed, it would have been all over, he couldn't have lifted a finger. He had to keep shoving everything off-center, not let himself find out how tired he was. He needed to keep himself keyed up and stretched tight to play the way he wanted to. It was work and a way of working.

But it was a drastic means and it worried his friends. It had got to the place where no one could tell how drunk he was unless he hadn't been drinking for a few hours. When it began to go out you could make a guess about how much it had been. The rest of the time you couldn't be sure whether he was drunk or just pre-occupied. He'd learned to handle the outward signs when he was playing with Morrison.

Smoke Jordan tried hard to get him to take it easier, maybe not play so much, maybe take a vacation, Florida's nice.

'Get yourself wheeled up and down like an icky banker?'

'Oh, I don't know,' Smoke said. 'It's all right. You wouldn't haf to get wheeled. Lay on the beach and look at the waves.'

'No Florida,' Rick said.

'If I wasn't working I'd get out of this town and go somewheres, boy, I'm telling you that.'

But it didn't do any good. Rick didn't leave New York all winter long, and he worked harder than he ever had when he had had a job. Every tenth record you'd pick up in those days would have some of that magnificent horn in it somewhere. Apparently anybody could call on him and he'd sit in just for the fun of it, just for the fun of riding along and pulling a whole band with him.

His own recording band, however, turned out to be a lost cause. He got the band together, one of the most exciting personnels anybody ever rounded up. Ten men, four black and six white. It was to be a co-operative, and they were signed by a company that was just getting its start and felt like taking a chance on something good. Rick had Smoke and Davis and Snowden and Jeff from Jeff's band, and La Porte from Morrison's, and Cohen from Freeman's, and Roland from Moss's, and Barrow and Lake from Deane's. The band was called Dick Rogers's Memphis Ten for the sake of anonymity, and it's too bad the record company went broke before any of their records were issued, because Dick Rogers's Memphis Ten was shaped like a winner.

But the company went broke. And Rick took it hard, because he had felt right about it. The thing he'd wanted to do ever since he could remember was to get a good band and make records that weren't held by anything. He got the band, that part worked out.

He showed up, icy-eyed, at Louie Galba's the night he found out the company had gone under. He pushed through the door and went to a table alone. He didn't have his trumpet with him; all he had was a flask which he fetched out of a pocket and laid on the table in front of him. It was about two-thirty. At three Jeff came in and Rick told him as much as he could.

'We ought to have expected it,' Jeff said. 'Same thing I told you a year ago when you wanted to try it. Only I thought this really looked good. Too damned bad.'

'You don't have to worry,' Rick said. 'You've got a band and you can make what you want, in a sort of way. Where does a white guy get, though? What can he do?'

'Do you wish you were playing in a band again?' Jeff said. 'Like Morrison's? Maybe you ought to go back. It's a good band. Good as any when you played in it.'

'I don't want to go back,' Rick said; 'but, at that, I wouldn't mind being regular in a good band, one that was good all the time, not just one chorus in ten. I don't know. I can't get along in a band. I used to work for Morrison, did you know that? — worked for him for five years.'

Jeff looked at him closely and didn't answer.

'I can't get along in a band,' Rick said. 'It . . . I don't know, it sort of weighs me down. I couldn't get along at Balboa. I worked down there once when I was a kid for a summer, and I couldn't get along from the first day. No use to try it again. I can't get along in a band. Gotta go now.'

He stood up, collected his flask, and pushed straight out the door. There was something about the way he walked. It wasn't stiff-legged, exactly, but it was on that style.

8

HE DIDN'T show up anywhere for three weeks. The boys were laying bets he was dead. Smoke forced himself through the morgue twice, looked over the whole display, tags and all. Then he called up all the jails. Not the right Martin. But he wouldn't give it up. He kept trying everything he could think of, and then one morning an old woman gave him a tip and he found him and put him in a cure.

It was one of those cures where they saturate you with alcohol and then pump you full of a preparation that gives you an allergy to alcohol. It makes a conflict. The forces for good do battle with the forces of evil and the patient has a time of it. The patient is expected to remember the conflict as long as he lives, and the assumption is that he'll never take a chance on another. He'd just prefer not to.

Smoke came to get Rick the day he was supposed to be released. He'd had his suit cleaned and he brought it along for him to wear home. He rang a bell in the waiting-room, and a man in a surgeon's smock came in and said thank heavens he'd come, they'd been trying every place they knew to get in touch with him or somebody that knew the patient.

'What's wrong?' Smoke said, wide-eyed. 'Couldn't he take the cure?'

It wasn't that. He took the cure fine, at least they

gave it to him, but he turned out not to be in such good shape in other respects. He had had a bad cold when he came in, and now it looked like either pneumonia or double pneumonia.

'You're a doctor, which do you think?' Smoke said, and the one in the smock said he was a special kind of doctor; he just gave alcohol and narcotics cures, and he wouldn't say anything for sure, but his guess was that that boy should be taken to a hospital; they had begun to think so two days before, but there wasn't anything to identify the patient, after Smoke took his suit, and they couldn't find anyone to give them an authorization.

'Why didn't you authorize yourself?' Smoke said. 'You didn't need to worry. I'd have paid you anyhow.'

'My own feeling is,' the cure doctor said, 'that we'd better get him out of here quick.'

He called an ambulance, and Smoke went in to see Rick.

It was a small room with white walls, one barred window, and a hospital bed. No other furniture, nothing to break. It was simply a cell, a place to suffer in while the conflict raged. The late sun poked through the bars. It was one of the first days of spring, a good day to ride on top of a bus, a rotten day for an ambulance.

Rick's head lay flat against the sheet; the covers were pinned close by his ears with huge safety pins, so that nothing but his head was outside.

His eyes flicked when Smoke came in. They stayed

open for a moment and burned like lighted rum. He twisted violently and the sheet tore a little where it was pinned. Then he lay perfectly still and moaned low, but didn't speak.

Smoke tiptoed to the side of the bed and whispered: 'Take it easy, baby; I'm going to get you out of here. It's a quack joint, and the doctor doesn't know his business from a hole in the ground. He's not even a doctor.'

Rick's eyes came open halfway and the flames jumped out when they caught the draft.

He looked up at Smoke and said: 'I worked for him, but I couldn't get along. Can't get along in a band.'

Smoke couldn't make out the words. 'Sure,' he said. 'Just forget it.'

He closed his eyes again. He had a three weeks' beard, and there was a bright red circle on each cheek. His hair fell in rings over his forehead. The prophet in his homeland is not supposed to be taken seriously. Let him cut loose and go someplace else, or have done with prophesying. What do we know about this young man with the beard and the spots on his cheeks, this young man pinned down in a strange bed in a barred room, out of his head with a fever? What do we know except that he had a way of doing a thing, and that he had a love of the thing so strong that he never in his life compromised it, or let it down, or forgot it?

Rick twisted sharply against the sheet, but this

time it didn't tear. His mouth was scarlet and he opened it and said: 'I don't see why we couldn't. Just call it the Memphis Ten or some name, same bunch all the time, do up a lot of good ones, all the ones we used to play.'

He said it, but the words he used didn't mean anything, and when Smoke bent down close to try to hear him he only heard sounds — sounds that should have meant: 'If I had been born into a different kind of world, at another place, in another time, everything changed, the name Martin might have lasted along with the names of the other devout ones, the ones who cared for music and put it down so that it's still good and always will be. But what chance has a jig-man got? He plays his little tune, and then it's over, and he alone can know what went into it. This is sad; but so is everything, and in the end there is another thing to say about it. The good thing, finally, is to lead a devoted life, even if it swings around and strikes you in the face.'

Smoke stayed there, close, trying to get anything he could, but the sounds just didn't mean anything.

The cure doctor came in with two ambulance men wearing white coats and carrying a stretcher between them. They took the pins out and turned back the covers and Rick lay quietly, his arms crossed unnaturally far over on his chest. The thing they had on him was a strait-jacket.

'Loosen it up and leave it on him,' one of the stretcher men said. 'This boy don't need restraining.'

They rolled him onto the stretcher and carried him to the ambulance. Smoke got in and sat beside him on a jump seat. They drove slowly between streets, but they put on a little speed at intersections and went across with the siren wide open.

The sun was in Rick's face. Smoke reached up and pulled down the blind. Then he settled back and said, 'I knew a guy once that took a cure and he said...' But he stopped it there because he suddenly knew that it wasn't getting over. He looked down and saw Rick's face. He watched, stunned, and while he was watching, Rick died. He could tell when it happened. There was a difference.

THE END

Sentry Editions